Wicked Games

Hope
Everly

Dedication

For my husband and my two incredible children,

Your unwavering love and support have been my anchor through every challenge, every setback, and every new beginning. When others doubted, you believed. Through chronic illness and now an entirely new path, you have stood beside me, lifting me up with your love, patience, and encouragement.

I am endlessly grateful for you. You are my strength, my inspiration, and my greatest joy.

I love you more than words can ever express.

For Aunty Ro Ro and Uncle John,

Thank you for always being there when I needed you most. Through the tears, the tough times, and the long ass phone calls, you've shown me unconditional love, patience, and kindness.

Some of my fondest memories live on your farm—school holiday escapes filled with laughter, comfort, and the kind of simple joy that stays with you forever.

Aunty Ro Ro, you were the first to introduce me to romance. From *Anne of Green Gables* to *Seven Brides for Seven Brothers* and *By the Light of the Silvery Moon*, your love for heartfelt stories lit a spark in me that still burns bright. You helped shape the hopeless romantic I am today and continue to inspire the emotion I pour into my writing.

Thank you both for being steady, loving role models—and for helping me believe in love, even when life made it hard to.

Acknowledgements

To Diana,

What started as a simple connection over a story turned into one of the most cherished friendships of my life. You have been more than just a reader, you've been my sounding board, my confidante, and my greatest source of encouragement when I doubted myself. Your endless support, unwavering belief in me, and love for this journey have meant more than words can ever express.

Your friendship is a gift, and your support is priceless. I am beyond grateful for you.

Trigger Warning

Hey, it's Noah. Before you dive into this book, I just wanna give you a heads-up—because some of the stuff in here? It's pretty heavy.

There's yelling. There's hitting. There's people who are meant to love you... but don't. There's stuff about being hurt in ways no kid—or anyone—should ever be. And sometimes, it's hard to breathe when you're reading it. Trust me, I know.

If you've ever felt scared in your own home, or like no one's listening, or like the world's just too loud—yeah, it gets that real in here. There's talk about abuse, violence, drugs, and bad memories that don't leave you alone.

So, if you need to take a break? Do it. If you need to put it down? That's okay too. Just know this story isn't about staying broken. It's about fighting your way out. It's about second chances—even when you don't think you'll get one.

You're not alone. Not ever.

—Noah

Wicked Games
The Playlist

Hey... it's Willow.

This playlist isn't just background music. It's the sound of everything I've been through, every scream I never let out, every tear I swallowed down, every moment I felt like giving up but didn't.

These songs are pieces of me. The chaos of growing up in a world that never felt safe. The confusion of wanting love and not knowing if I deserve it. The pull of two very different men, one who made me feel wanted, and one who made me feel seen.

You'll hear the pain I tried to hide. The trust I'm scared to give. The war inside my head every time I let someone get too close. But somewhere in all of it, you'll hear hope, too. A spark. A second chance.

So, if you've ever felt like the world forgot you... If you've ever been broken, bruised, or barely holding on... This is for you. Plug in. Turn it up. And let yourself feel it, even the messy parts. We're not alone anymore.

Willow

- **Wicked Game** – Jessie Villa
- **Control** – Halsey
- **I Found** – Amber Run
- **Lovely** – Billie Eilish & Khalid
- **Breathe Me** – Sia
- **Run to You** – Pentatonix
- **Youth** – Daughter
- **Hurt** – Nine Inch Nails
- **Without Me** – Halsey
- **Creep (Acoustic)** – Radiohead
- **Start a War** – Klergy & Valerie Broussard
- **Unsteady** – X Ambassadors
- **Mad World** – Gary Jules
- **The Night We Met** – Lord Huron
- **Silhouette** – Aquilo
- **Earned It** – The Weeknd
- **All I Want** – Kodaline
- **Love the Way You Lie (Part II)** – Rihanna ft. Eminem
- **Skinny Love** –Birdy version
- **Take Me to Church** – Hozier

Chapter 1
Willow

The alley was cold and damp—the kind of cold that settled deep into your bones, no matter how many layers you wore. It reeked of stale smoke and piss, the scent clinging to cracked bricks and broken pavement like it had claimed the place long ago. The walls around me were splattered with chaotic graffiti—bright, angry colors now faded and bleeding into one another, like ghosts of people who once tried to be seen but were long forgotten.

I leaned back against the brick wall, the rough surface pressing into my shoulder blades as the last light of day stretched tired shadows across my feet. My posture was casual—or at least, that's what I hoped it looked like. But underneath, I was tired. Tired in that way that never really leaves. The kind of tired that comes from surviving, not sleeping.

My clothes hung off me, dark and oversized, easy to hide in, easy to forget. My bright pink hair was the only color on me— the last piece of rebellion I hadn't let the world strip away.

The hum of the street echoed in the distance—cars rolling by, voices arguing, laughing, surviving. All of it dulled into a low background noise that never truly stopped.

In front of me stood Razor.

She leaned against the opposite wall like she owned the damn alley, exhaling slow, deliberate drags of smoke, like she had nothing and everything to prove. Her wild purple hair was pulled back messily, like she didn't care how it looked—and somehow that only made her look more dangerous.

Her hazel eyes flicked over me, narrowed and sharp. Always watching. Always calculating. She didn't say anything, but she didn't have to.

Razor was the kind of girl you didn't mess with unless you had a death wish. The scars across her arms and face weren't just from fights—they were reminders. Warnings. She carried her story in blood and broken bones, and people around here respected that.

Hell, they feared her.

And I didn't blame them.

I'd heard the whispers. The stories. The one about the guy who tried to grab her outside the club last winter and ended up with a blade between his ribs. No one ever confirmed it, but in a place like this? Silence was confirmation.

My gaze lingered on her, "Slamming body," I thought to myself, a wry grin tugging at my lips. Tough as nails, with a stare that could make any enemy weak at the knees.

But that wasn't me. No matter how many times I wished I could be like Razor, I wasn't. Razor had it all—fearlessness, respect, a reputation that demanded attention. I couldn't help but feel small in comparison.

I wondering how I always ended up around people like her. Maybe it was because I understood what it meant to be backed into a corner. Maybe because, deep down, I knew I was similar to her—only quieter, less lethal about it.

Less smoke. More scars no one could see.

The other figure, Blaze, was a different kind of intimidating. Cool, collected, and always seemed to have a buzz that never quite wore off. Her pale blue hair and dark makeup only emphasized her otherworldly aura. She leaned back against the brick, her posture relaxed, but there was a sharpness to her presence. Chill incarnate, like nothing in the world could touch her.

Most of the district worshipped her. Her charm was magnetic, her smile rare and coveted.

I watched Blaze for a moment, catching the way her lips curled into a rare smile as she looked out at the world with a certain detachment—as if nothing could touch her. She was the kind of person who could be your best friend one minute and your worst enemy the next. Behind those eyes was a coldness, a sharpness I knew better than to provoke.

But even with the allure of Razor's strength and Blaze's cold confidence—no matter how much I wished—I knew I wasn't quite like them. They were far more polished, far more dangerous, far more intimidating than I could ever be. I was just... me. A girl who did what she had to, even when it meant losing myself a little more every day.

I glanced down at myself, barely standing out between these two forces of nature. Seventeen, unimpressive, and somehow surviving. I laughed under my breath. "Yeah, the far less impressive one," I said softly, eyes on the cracked pavement.

I wasn't fierce. I wasn't feared. But I'd managed to stick around, to survive in a world as harsh as the streets Razor and Blaze ruled. I couldn't say why I was friends with them—only that they were my only anchor in a life that offered little else. Without them, I wasn't sure how long I would have lasted.

A sharp car engine noise snapped me out of my thoughts, and I looked toward the nearby apartment complex. It loomed like a tired sentinel—reddish bricks stained by years of neglect. Home.

I couldn't help but let out a dry, sarcastic chuckle. That's what they told me to call it.

I'd lived there for two years now, and every day felt like a reminder that I wasn't truly wanted—not by the people who lived there, not by anyone really. I didn't know why I was still here, in this dump, with people who barely acknowledged me. Maybe... maybe I just needed someone to tell me I was worth something.

I pushed myself off the wall and walked down the cracked pavement, my steps dragging. Approaching the building, I could see the windows above me, their glass dull with grime. I'd be back at my foster home in a minute, but that didn't mean I was looking forward to it. My "family," if I could even call them that, was a joke.

The front door creaked open, and stale cigarette smoke and cheap liquor hit me. There was Barbara—my so-called foster mother—sitting at the kitchen table, her thin lips curled into a permanent sneer. Beside her, Noah—small, scrappy, and always in trouble—sat motionless, emotionless like a zombie in the corner. Meanwhile, Brandy, the short, fair-haired teenager, shouted fire in her eyes.

I had tried to protect Noah from it, but it never worked. He was always the one caught in the messes I had to clean up.

I crossed my arms and leaned against the doorframe, letting out a heavy sigh.

This is my family, I thought bitterly, watching the scene unfold. This is my foster home.

Barb was a woman who'd long given up pretending to be a caring mother. She saw her kids as paychecks—money to spend on alcohol, gambling, drugs, anything that kept her numb. She looked like she spent every dollar that way too—skin like old leather, shoulder-length hair that hadn't been done in decades. Barb didn't care about us. She barely cared about herself.

Maybe that's why we were all so lost—because no one ever cared enough to show us the way.

Noah blinked slowly, eyes fixed on some invisible spot on the wall. He always got like this when there were fights. Still. Silent. Like if he didn't move, the noise wouldn't touch him. Like he could make himself disappear.

It broke my heart every damn time. Because I knew that version of him wasn't real.

Noah was the loud one. The bright one. The kid who talks too fast when he's excited, who laughs with his whole body, who makes up the dumbest jokes just to see me roll my eyes. He was light in a place that's seen too much dark.

But when things got loud, when voices rose, when fists clenched and the air grew tight with tension, he vanished. Gone. That confident, goofy spark dimmed, and what was left was this hollowed-out shell.

And he wouldn't talk about why. Not really. He just shut down, crawled deep inside himself, and locked the door behind him.

I didn't know what happened before he got to me, but I saw the scars and knew it was bad—bad enough that arguments didn't sound like noise to him, but like danger.

No matter how many times I told him he was safe now… part of him didn't believe it. Maybe part of me didn't either. Because in this world? Safety feels like a lie we keep trying to sell ourselves.

But I'd keep trying.

Because Noah deserved more than silence and fear.

He deserved to be a kid. To stay that bright, loud, messy little light. Even if I had to fight the world to protect it.

I was snapped back as Brandy jabbed a finger at Barb, voice rising. "You only care about the paycheck!" she shouted, anger crackling like a live wire.

Barb laughed—a cold, sharp sound that cut through the room. "And what are you gonna do about it?" she shot back in that raspy voice, years of heavy smoking thick in every word. "Run to the department? You think they'll believe you?"

Brandy's anger faltered, posture deflating. Barb's smirk widened, savoring every retort and the defeat etched on Brandy's face.

"That temper of yours has already burned through five homes. They'll ship you off to the dorms so fast your head will spin."

There it was—the threat that ended every argument.

The dorms. Even saying it made my stomach twist. It wasn't a home. It was the last stop—the end of the road for kids like us, the ones no one picked, the ones passed around too many times or who gave up trying to be lovable.

You know how dogs end up in pounds when no one wants them? That's what the dorms were for foster kids. A holding cell. Cold. Cramped. Forgotten.

Where they put us when there was nowhere else to go.

The air always smelled like bleach and something sour underneath—as if they tried to scrub out the truth but couldn't quite get rid of it. Thin mattresses, locked doors, screaming at all hours. You learned fast not to cry. Not because no one cared, but because someone might hear—and the ones who heard were often worse than the ones who didn't.

I stopped hoping for a real bed. A real family. Even kindness started to feel suspicious—like a trick.

The dorms didn't break me all at once. They did it slowly. Quietly. One disappointment at a time.

Until I started to believe what the walls whispered:

You're not wanted. You never were.

I only spent a short time there—a couple months transitioning between homes. But it was enough.

Barb? Barb was the home I transitioned to.

"Enough!" I snapped, breaking from my spiraling thoughts, stepping forward. "Can you at least stop fighting in front of Noah? You know it upsets him."

Barb waved me off with a lazy hand. "Toughens him up," she muttered. I clenched my jaw but didn't argue. There was no winning with her.

I turned away, retreating to my room. I wasn't sticking around for more of this. I couldn't.

The door slammed behind me, echoing through the apartment. I leaned against it, the weight pressing down. I didn't know what I was doing anymore, but I knew one thing for sure:

I wasn't going to let this place break me.

I closed my eyes, trying to block out the kitchen noise. As I breathed in the stale air of my room, I wondered how much longer I could keep going—how much longer I could survive in a world that seemed determined to tear me apart.

Slowly, I opened my eyes and sighed, taking in the cluttered room. Papers and clothes littered the floor, the bed barely visible beneath discarded garments. Jake and Summer were tangled in each other's arms, oblivious.

I coughed loudly, crossing my arms.

Jake turned, irritation clear. "Can't you see we're busy?" he snapped.

"I can," I shot back flatly. "Now I'll see myself out."

Closing the door behind me, I sighed heavily.

This was my life—a balancing act between chaos and survival.

And it was about to get so much worse.

"I suppose I'll go back out," I muttered, rolling my eyes.

I shuffled toward the front door, my sneakers scuffing against the floor.

Chapter 2
Willow

The corridor was as dreary as the apartment I'd just left—narrow, uninviting, with peeling wallpaper and faint stains marring the worn carpet. Razor and Blaze leaned against the wall, idly smoking, their shadows melting into the gloom. I hesitated, uncertain if I was invisible or just being ignored.

Razor broke the silence, impatience sharp in her voice as she turned to me. "I'm hungry. We ain't getting our split till Friday."

Blaze shrugged, flicking ash from her cigarette.

"Yeah, whatever. I'll survive. Don't expect me to lift a finger."

Their stares weighed on me like a physical force. I sighed, voice barely above a whisper. "I just used the last of my cash on milk and bread."

Why I said that, I didn't know. I knew how this went. Always did. There was only one outcome.

Razor snorted, eyes narrowing with disbelief. "I don't want excuses, Willow. Just get it done. You know the drill."

What response could I give? It wasn't a question, it was a command. Saying no wasn't an option. Walking away wasn't something I had the guts for.

I turned, footsteps quickening down the creaking hall. The old building groaned around me, whispering secrets I didn't want to hear. Past the rickety stairs and into the cold evening air.

The alley behind the building was dull, grimy, and littered with rubbish. A rusty dumpster overflowed in the corner, sending up the stench of rotten food and stale beer—air thick, as if it had been breathed and rebreathed for years. The ground felt ready to swallow me whole as I hurried forward, eyes scanning for a place to hide, knowing what came next. Razor's orders weren't questions—they were laws.

This was routine now. I no longer thought, just obeyed. Razor had a way of getting what she wanted, sending me where she needed without hesitation. No one crossed Razor. No one asked questions. The rules were simple: Razor wanted it, Razor got it.

I slipped through the alley, searching for a safe spot, avoiding anyone's gaze as I moved toward my destination.

The corner store's dim neon lights flickered ahead—a place I knew too well. My fingers brushed my jacket pocket, feeling the crumpled, empty packet—the evidence of theft from months ago. I glanced around, making sure no one watched, before stepping inside.

The store was quiet, too quiet. The fluorescent lights hummed overhead as I moved down the aisles, picking up small items—a chocolate bar, a can of beans—nothing too obvious. I grabbed a bag of chips for Blaze and a couple things for Razor, careful to choose their favourites. I didn't want to steal tonight, but I didn't have a choice.

Suddenly, the shopkeeper's voice cut through the silence like a knife. "Oi! It's you!"

I froze. His eyes burned into mine with angry recognition. My stomach dropped. I swallowed hard, trying to steady my nerves.

"How dare you show your face in here again?" he spat, stepping toward me.

Before I could think, I spun around and bolted for the door, heart hammering. The shopkeeper yelled after me, but I didn't stop—not with Razor's demands hanging over me.

I sprinted down the alley, breath ragged, heart pounding. Was it the fear of getting caught? The stolen goods? Or the thought of Razor's wrath if I failed?

I ducked behind a stack of old boxes, a hiding spot I'd noticed earlier, peeking through the cracks. After a few tense moments, I whispered,
"I think he's gone."

I leaned back against the wall, the weight of relief pressing down. "I don't think he saw me come down the alley," I breathed, letting my guard drop.

Then, a voice slithered out of the shadows behind me—cold and smooth. "I wouldn't speak too soon, love."

Every hair on my body stood on end. I spun around, heart hammering, and saw him:

A tall, broad thug, reeking of stale tobacco and cheap whiskey. His grin was wide, yellowed, far from friendly. It was dangerous.

The kind of smile that feeds on fear.

I couldn't breathe.

"What's a pretty thing like you doing walking these back alleys?" he asked, voice slick with false charm that made my skin crawl.

I opened my mouth but no words came. My throat clenched tight. I was frozen—every muscle seized by fear that wrapped around my chest, stealing my breath and my voice.

"I'm talking to you," he snapped, cold and cruel, stepping closer. The air thickened with threat. My knees wobbled, hands trembling.

He was sizing me up like I was meat. I wanted to run. Damn it, I wanted to run. But my feet were cemented to the ground by panic and memories—by knowing sometimes you don't get away.

Then, a voice cut through the tension—strong and familiar, making my heart leap for a different reason.

"Larry, you wouldn't be harassing our girl, would you?"

The thug's face changed instantly. That smug grin vanished as two shadows stepped into the alley's mouth—Razor and Blaze.

They didn't speak. Didn't need to. Their presence was the threat.

Razor stood like a queen on a battlefield, back straight, chin high, eyes sharp and cold—twin blades of ice. She didn't raise her voice. Her silence was enough.

Beside her, Blaze was a storm barely held back. Her fists clenched tight enough to show white knuckles, chest rising and falling with shallow breaths. This was no posture. This was real. Blaze was fire and fury, every muscle wound tight like a weapon waiting to strike.

She wasn't the warning. She was the consequence.

And for the first time, I felt a flicker of safety—not because I was safe, but because they were here.

The thug stammered, bravado crumbling. "Oh, hey, Razor. Didn't know she was with you."

Razor's smile was tight. "Well, that's good to know. Now, what are you still doing here?"

Realizing his mistake, the thug took off, vanishing into the shadows without another word.

I exhaled the breath I didn't know I'd been holding. Razor and Blaze moved past me, eyes sharp with suspicion but their focus back on me.

"Why do you let guys like that get so close?" Razor asked sternly, though a hint of concern softened her tone.

I hesitated. Pulling at my shirt sleeve, "I'm just trying to stay out of trouble."

Razor gave a half-smile. "That's why you're with us. We keep you safe."

I didn't respond. I wasn't sure I believed that anymore. They took care of me, yes, but there was always a price. Always a catch.

After a long silence, Razor spoke again as they snatched the stolen items from my arms. "You did good, Willow. After we eat, we scout."

A lump formed in my throat at her words. I nodded, face neutral, but inside unease churned. I never liked to scout.

Chapter 3
Willow

Darkness settled heavily over us. When the meal was done, the mission began. The streets grew quieter, their pulse fading as we slipped deeper into the city's underbelly.

The alley we entered was cloaked in shadows, the only light seeping through cracks between the old brick buildings, casting jagged shapes on the damp pavement. The graffiti wasn't the bold, careless scrawls of neighborhood kids; it was a map of survival, coded marks left by those who had walked this path before us.

The cold pavement bit into my skin as I lay down, exhaustion clawing at my muscles, threatening to consume me entirely. I clenched my jaw, forcing my focus back to the world around me. Vulnerability wasn't an option—not here.

Razor's voice cut through the silence like a whip. "Now, Willow."

I groaned weakly, the weight of my situation pressing heavily on my chest. "Ohhhh... help!" My voice was barely above a whimper at first, but desperation pushed it louder. "SOMEONE HELP!"

Footsteps echoed from the mouth of the alley. A well-dressed man hurried toward me, his concerned gaze scanning the scene. "Are you okay, Miss?" he asked, crouching beside me. His voice carried genuine concern—a rare find in this part of town.

Before I could even speak, Razor and Blaze emerged from the shadows like creatures born of darkness itself.

Razor's blade caught the faint light as it spun in her fingers, her face sharp lines and cold fury. She didn't blink—just stepped forward with that same quiet malice she wore like a second skin.

Blaze followed close behind, cracking her knuckles beneath the weight of her brass knuckles. The sound was loud and deliberate in the tight space of the alley. It was a threat. A promise.

"You can't help her," Razor hissed, eyes locked on the man who had only tried to do the right thing. Her voice was smooth, seductive, but beneath it bled venom. "But you can help us."

A beat of silence.

"By giving us your wallet."

I watched the man freeze, a flicker of panic flashing in his eyes. He glanced over his shoulder—toward the street, toward freedom—but it was too late. We'd boxed him in. He knew it. We all did.

Blaze stepped forward and slammed her fist into her palm, a slow, steady rhythm that made my stomach turn. It echoed off the alley walls—each sound a cruel drumbeat counting down the seconds he had left to resist.

I scrambled to my feet, brushing dirt from my jeans with shaky hands. My heart thundered like footsteps in an empty hall, each beat louder than my breath. My chest tightening like it always did in moments like this.

I never felt easy about doing this.

Because it wasn't me. I hated it. Every damn second of it.

This man didn't deserve it. He was just trying to help. Just trying to be kind in a world that chews kindness up and spits it out. But kindness doesn't get you far here. And Razor and Blaze?

They were my protection in a life that never handed me any. I couldn't afford to lose that.

So I stood there. Silent. Sick. Complicit.

When the man finally handed over his wallet with shaking hands, Razor snatched it with a smirk—as if taking back something that was always owed. Blaze laughed—sharp and mean—the sound slicing through me like glass. It made my skin crawl.

"Let's get out of here before the cops show up," I said shakily. I didn't look at the man again. I couldn't. We disappeared into the night like ghosts, like cowards.

Razor and Blaze walked ahead, triumphant and loud, their laughter ringing down the alley like they'd won something.

I followed behind, dragging the weight of my guilt with every step. Because maybe they were untouchable.

But I wasn't.

And every time we did this, I lost a little more of myself.

What choice did I have? In this world, you're either protected—or you're prey.

Tonight, I chose not to be the latter. Even if it meant becoming someone I barely recognized.

Back at the apartment, Razor tossed a wad of cash onto the table, a triumphant grin spreading across her face. "We hit the jackpot with this one. Three hundred bucks and a thirty-dollar gift card."

Blaze whooped with excitement. "Man, I'm gonna have a good night tonight!"

"And here," Razor tossed the gift card to me. "You can have this, Willow."

I caught it hesitantly, staring at the small plastic rectangle. It felt more like a bribe than a gift—a token meant to pacify me while they reaped all the rewards.

Razor leaned back, lighting a cigarette. "Acid's got a big job planned—a jewelry heist. He wants our help."

Blaze was instantly on board, but my stomach sank. My voice trembled as I spoke. "I don't really want to do that, Razor."

Her eyes narrowed dangerously. "And why not?"

"This... it's serious," I stammered. "If we get caught, it's not just a slap on the wrist. It's real time."

Razor leaned in close, her gaze piercing through me like a blade. "You know about the job now. You're doing it. End of story."

I bit my lip, the taste of defeat bitter in my mouth. "Okay," I whispered. I didn't have a choice. Razor's shadow loomed too large over my life, and the thought of defying her was more terrifying than the crime itself.

Chapter 4
Willow

Later, I wandered through another dark alley, the gift card still clenched in my hand. The promise of a momentary escape teased the edges of my thoughts. But Ray's voice shattered the fragile quiet.

"Hey, Dimples."

I rolled my eyes, heart sinking. Ray was just another predator in a world full of them—his charm slick and poisonous. He made my skin crawl before he even spoke.

He carried himself with smug arrogance, born from years of intimidation and getting his way. His greasy dark blue hair was slicked to one side—a desperate attempt at personality that only highlighted the deep lines of a face hardened by shady dealings. His beady black eyes darted around, calculating, sizing up everything and everyone like they were already his to take.

His expensive clothes looked wrong on him, like he was playing dress-up in a life that wasn't his. Cheap cologne clung to him, masking something far more unpleasant underneath. When he smirked, it was never amusement—it was cold satisfaction, the smile of someone who enjoyed holding others at his mercy.

I'd seen men like Ray before: men who took and took until nothing was left. He didn't need to raise his voice. His presence alone made my stomach turn.

"What do you want, Ray?" I clenched my fists, fighting the revulsion burning in my gut.

"Oh, don't play coy." He stepped into my space, claiming it like his own. His tone darkened. "Your little brother owes me. If you don't want me to take it out on him, you know what you need to do."

Rage flared. "Leave Noah alone!" I snapped, voice trembling.

Ray smirked, clearly enjoying my anger. "That's up to you, sweetheart. You know the deal."

I pressed the $30 gift card into his calloused hand. "A $30 gift card. Payment for whatever Noah took."

He let out a low, cruel laugh that sent chills down my spine. Leaning in close, his breath hot against my cheek, he whispered with malice, "I'm not taking that." His lips twisted. "I don't need your money, Dimples."

His gaze slid over me, slow and deliberate, the air thickening between us.

"But that sweet ass of yours..." He licked his lips, eyes gleaming as he eyed me up and down. "Now, that's a different kind of payment."

I shuddered—not from the cold, but from something darker. Him. Ray.

There was no talking my way out. No kindness to soften him. I knew it in his calculating eyes, in the way he moved—too calm, too certain.

My mind scrambled: Say something. Buy time. Run. Fight.

I glanced around the alley—heart pounding. The walls felt like a trap. I looked toward the street, hoping for a miracle. But nothing. No footsteps. No headlights. No help.

Just silence. And him. Ray.

But I already knew, on these streets, his name was whispered in warning—second only to Razor and Acid. No one dared cross him, not even them. Interrupting Ray when he was collecting was unthinkable.

His name twisted my stomach. He wasn't just some guy. He was my history—the shadow I could never outrun.

I didn't need to wonder what he was capable of. I already knew. And that was the worst part.

No delaying. No escape.

Only endurance. Only survival.

And I wasn't sure how much I had left.

A heavy sigh escaped me, weighed down by resignation.

"Stop wasting my time," he snapped, the air crackling with tension. "If you keep talking, I'll put that mouth of yours to better use. Your chatter only drags this out."

My gaze dropped. My stomach churned as I dragged myself deeper into the alley, each step defying the scream inside. I clung to one thought: This was for Noah. It had to be.

Ray's hand slammed into my lower back, shoving me forward. I stumbled, catching the cold, damp bricks—biting through my thin shirt like knives.

Then he was on me.

His body pressed tight, suffocating any space to breathe. His breath hot and unwanted on my neck. His hands roamed greedily, fingers digging into places they didn't belong.

My skin crawled. But I didn't scream. I'd learned screaming never helped.

So I did what I always did—I left. Not physically, but in my head.

Desperate for escape, my eyes darted around. That's when I saw it.

A faded butterfly, cracked and half-hidden behind grime and peeling paint—streaks of purple and pink still clinging stubbornly to the wall.

Time had worn it down, scraped it away, but it was still there—still trying to be something beautiful in a place that never cared.

I clung to that image like a lifeline.

Ray's sweat and cheap cologne flooded my senses, trying to drag me under. But I fought it. I stared at the broken butterfly and imagined flying—far away.

A life where I wasn't trapped in alleys.

Where I wasn't touched without permission.

Where I wasn't owned.

A life where I was free.

For a moment, I let myself believe that life might exist. Even if it didn't. Even if I'd never live it.

I had to believe something—because if I didn't, I wouldn't survive this.

What had I done to end up here?

The thought circled like a noose tightening. What wrong turn? What mistakes led me here?

Was this punishment? Or just the fate of another forgotten girl chewed up and spat out by a broken world?

I'd turn eighteen soon.

Maybe then I could disappear—leave Barb, leave everything. Maybe take Noah and run. Just the two of us, living in a busted car, stealing food, hiding in motels—petty crimes and cheap dreams. Us against the world.

Or maybe I still clung to fantasies I should've outgrown, like those movies I snuck to watch after midnight—Pretty Woman, that stupid, beautiful lie.

A rich man would find me. See past the dirt, the bruises, the shame clinging to my skin. Lift me out of this life. Shower me with gifts. Make me feel worthy.

And we'd live happily ever after.

Right.

But reality crashed down harder than Ray's weight on me.

This was my life. Doing things I swore I never would. Letting go of pieces of myself just to survive.

Bread. Milk. Survival.

That was the cost.

A single tear slipped down my cheek, hot with shame. I hated myself for still hoping, still wanting someone to see me when no one ever did.

His voice shattered the silence, dragging me back.

"Well, sweetheart," Ray oozed cruel satisfaction, "looks like you haven't lost your touch."

I didn't move. Didn't flinch. I stared past him, pretending I was somewhere else.

His lips curled, slow and repulsive, as his tongue flicked across them like tasting control. His eyes scanned me like I was a thing—nothing more than a transaction.

"I'm gonna have to find new ways to make Noah owe me."

The words punched me in the gut. Bile rose, but I swallowed it. For Noah.

He leaned in, so close I could smell whiskey, cheap cologne, sweat. I wanted to turn away. I couldn't.

Then, like some twisted final move—like breaking me wasn't enough—he dragged the tip of his tongue up the tear on my cheek.

I stopped breathing. My body froze in a silent scream.

It wasn't just disgusting—it was deliberate. A sick, slow performance meant to humiliate and own me deeper than skin.

And it worked.

In that moment, I wasn't a person. I was a thing—a plaything for his power, something to use and discard.

But it meant everything to me.

Because that quiet act was when something inside me broke.

Not the loud, screaming break.

The quiet kind—the kind where a piece of yourself slips away, and you're too numb to reach for it.

I wanted to scream. To fight. But I couldn't move or speak. Could barely hold on to the idea of me.

Maybe that was his goal.

To leave me standing there—hollow, ashamed, wearing silence like a second skin.

"Well, Dimples," he muttered, the nickname dripping like a slur, "I've got things to take care of. Don't make me wait too long."

He pulled back, straightened his jacket like he hadn't just broken something sacred, and walked off. His boots echoed down the alley like gunshots.

I stayed frozen, breath shallow, eyes fixed on the crumbling wall.

Still. Silent. Shattered. But not destroyed. Not yet.

By night's end, I was alone—broken and ashamed. Ray vanished into darkness, and I was left to piece together what remained of my pride. Tears streaked my face as I leaned against the cold, unforgiving bricks.

This was my life—the one I had to survive and endure for Noah. I didn't care much anymore, but I'd do anything for him. Even this.

Someday, I promised myself, I'd find a way out. Away from Ray, away from the debt and fear. I'd give Noah a chance at better.

But for now, survival was all I had.

Chapter 5
Willow

The memory of the promise lingered as I stood in the fluorescent-lit sports store. Harsh lights flickered overhead, casting sharp shadows across rows of neatly stacked merchandise. The gift card burned in my pocket, its edges crinkled in my grip. My eyes scanned the aisles until they landed on the basketballs.

Noah's basketball.

His last one had been popped by local bullies. For days, I watched him tear up over it. That helplessness—it killed me. But here was a chance to fix one small thing.

I picked out a new ball, its glossy surface catching the light. Just picturing the relief on Noah's face loosened the tightness in my chest.

He was a good kid. Always trying to stay strong, even when life kept dealing us the worst hands. I couldn't fix everything for him—but this? This, I could do.

I thought of the groceries we needed. This meant sacrificing some essentials. A sigh slipped out. The rest of the card would go to bread, milk, whatever basics we could stretch. Still, I turned toward the cashier, the weight of that orange ball oddly grounding.

The kitchen greeted me with its usual gloom—small, cluttered, heavy with the stale scent of smoke and beer. It barely fit two, let alone all five of us. Noah sat slouched at the table, his frame too small for all the weight he carried. His eyes were dull, tired. Like he'd been waiting for something that never came.

"Hey, buddy." I tried for cheer. "Where's Barb?"

"She went to the casino. Said she feels lucky."

A bitter laugh tried to claw its way up, but I swallowed it. Perfect. Just what we needed.

I reached into the bag and pulled out the basketball. Its bright orange surface stood out in our grey world.

"Got you something. Didn't want to give it to you in front of her. Thought you could use a new one."

His eyes widened, hands curling around the ball like it was sacred. "Oh my gosh, thank you so much, Wills."

"Just... keep it out of sight, alright? Barb will only make things harder."

He nodded quickly and bounced the ball a couple times. The rhythmic thump filled the silence.

I took a deep breath. "Noah, we need to talk."

His smile faded. "What did I do?"

"It's not that. I just—" I folded my arms, unsure how to begin. "You've gotta stop taking stuff from Ray."

He shifted in his chair, confused. "But he's just trying to help."

"No, Noah. People like Ray don't help for free. They always want something in return. There's always a price."

His brow furrowed. "What does he want? What price?"

I hesitated, trying to push down the fear clawing at my insides. "Doesn't matter. I've handled it. But I need you to promise—no more accepting anything from him."

His gaze held mine. He nodded. "Promise."

And that mattered.

Promises meant everything to us. Not just words. Not anymore. Not after all the ones that had broken us. We'd laid side by side too many nights, whispering stories of trust lost and hope betrayed. So when we made a promise, it wasn't casual. It was sacred.

Between us, promises were unbreakable.

Relief loosened something tight inside me. "Thanks, Noah."

He grinned, bounced the ball again. "I'm gonna shoot some hoops."

"Don't be too long, it's dark out."

The door slammed behind him, the echo lingering. I yawned and stretched. "Big day tomorrow," I muttered. "Really don't want to do it."

The bedroom was cramped, barely enough space for the three of us sharing it. Brandy and Summer were already in bed, breathing soft and even. I stood at the doorway, watching the streetlight spill dim gold through the blinds.

I changed into pajamas and slipped under the thin blanket. Still, sleep didn't come.

What if we got caught tomorrow?

What if this was the end of the line?

Jail wasn't like here. Here, at least, I had some control. Out there—I'd be prey. Vulnerable.

Razor wouldn't take a no. She'd see it as betrayal. And betrayal? That never ended well.

"Damned if I do, damned if I don't," I whispered. "Cops won't kill me... but the inmates might."

I squeezed my eyes shut.

Fuck my life.

Chapter 6
Willow

The kitchen was cramped, dimly lit, and silent except for the low hum of the refrigerator. My fingers pressed against the cold countertop as I moved through the motions. Crack. Plop. Eggs hit the bowl. Flour sifted through my fingers. It wasn't much, but it was something.

Pancakes.

Noah's favorite.

A faint smile crept onto my lips. I'd stretched what was left on the voucher to buy the ingredients. Just enough to make a morning feel special with some spare change left.

"I hope we don't get caught today." The words slipped out, heavier than expected. Razor and Blaze were counting on me. I didn't want to be doing this, but choices had run out.

I flipped the last pancake onto the stack, golden and warm. Butter glistened in the soft yellow light. For a moment, the kitchen didn't feel like a cage. Just a quiet place holding onto something good.

Noah stirred in his bed tucked into the corner. His freckled face, still relaxed in sleep, made the chaos seem distant—like something we could outrun.

"Breakfast is ready," I said, setting the plate down carefully, like it might shatter.

He blinked awake, scrambled to his feet, the smell pulling him in. "You made pancakes?"

"Sure did, buddy."

His face lit up. "Is that really them?"

"Yep. Your favorite."

He was already digging in, fork tapping against the chipped plate. "I haven't had these in forever."

"Hopefully after today, we can have them more often." I tried to sound hopeful, though my chest tightened around the lie.

He paused, mid-bite. "What's happening today?"

I exhaled slowly. "Just helping Razor and Blaze with something. A job. If it works, we'll be in better shape."

His brow furrowed. "What if it doesn't?"

"It will." I forced a smile. "I just have to keep them happy. They'll look after me."

The words rang false, even to me. But he nodded, trusting me the way kids always do.

"Good. I want pancakes every day."

I chuckled. "You and me both."

We sat for a little longer, him eating, me watching. For a minute, it felt like normal. Like safe.

"I'm heading out," I said, standing. "If Barb asks, tell her I'll be back tonight."

He nodded without looking up.

I slipped on my jacket, the weight of it pressing down harder than usual. Razor and Blaze wouldn't wait.

At the door, I hesitated and turned.

Noah sat bathed in the soft light, fork in hand, mouth full, mid-laugh. A small universe of peace wrapped around him. His messy orange hair hung over his forehead, wild and perfect. Freckles scattered like constellations across his cheeks. Clothes too big, sleeves swallowed his arms—donation-bin remnants Barb had picked out. Somehow, he made them beautiful.

He looked like a little boy still believing the world was good.

He shouldn't have to live like this. None of us should.

The smile tugging at my lips felt wrong. My chest ached, and I held the moment like something sacred. Memorizing it. In case I needed to remember him like this.

God, I hope I don't have to.

Chapter 7
Willow

The city streets greeted me with their usual chaos—honking cars, distant voices blending into a low hum, and the steady rhythm of my boots on cracked pavement. It felt colder than usual. I tugged my jacket tighter. The fabric offered little protection from the chill seeping into my bones.

By the time I reached the alley, Razor and Blaze were already there, looming like shadows beneath layers of peeling graffiti. The tension was palpable—thick, biting, electric. I took a breath, hoping the night air would steady my nerves.

"You guys ready?" Razor's voice cut through the silence, calm and edged like a blade.

Blaze's eyes flicked to the side. "Hell yeah. If this works out, I could get high every day—on the good stuff."

Razor let out a short laugh. No humor in it.

I shifted, fists tightening at my sides. No turning back now.

"What about you, Willow?" Razor's tone sharpened, testing.

I shrugged. "I just want enough to make pancakes every morning. Maybe get Noah a new basketball kit."

Blaze scoffed. Razor smirked. "You're so simple."

Heat crawled into my cheeks. But I held her gaze. This wasn't about me.

"We'll get enough," Razor said, grin spreading. "Hell, you could have a personal chef flipping those pancakes."

Before I could answer, footsteps echoed. Acid and Butch emerged from the shadows, their presence thick like smoke. I dropped my eyes, trying to hide the tension coiling in my gut.

I avoided them whenever I could. Not because I wasn't afraid—because I was. Deeply.

They weren't just mean. They were cruel. Sadistic. The kind of people who hurt for fun.

Just seeing them made my stomach knot. Every part of me went still, on alert. Prey sensing predators.

Ink covered them—tattoos crawling up their necks like something alive, something poisonous. Every mark a warning. And it worked.

They walked like the world belonged to them, like they planned to take whatever hadn't already been given—and break it in the process.

Razor and Acid had this… thing. Toxic. Volatile. One moment tangled together like lifelines. The next, screaming threats and smashing bottles. Like watching someone play with matches next to a fuel tank.

Butch was a different kind of dangerous.

Massive. Silent. Like someone carved him from concrete and forgot to give him a soul. He didn't talk much—but when his eyes locked on you, it was like being pinned under a truck. You knew he was measuring your worth. Deciding if you were worth crushing.

His gaze landed on me, cold and sharp. I swallowed. Hard. My throat still felt like it was closing.

I couldn't move. Couldn't breathe.

Because in their world, weakness was blood in the water.

And I couldn't afford to bleed.

"So, what's the plan?" My voice came steadier than I felt, deliberately looking at Acid, trying to deflect Butch's focus.

Acid didn't waste time. "Razor and I go in first. You're out front—keep watch. Yell if you see anything. Butch and Blaze hit the display cabinets. Razor and I handle the safe."

I nodded, though my stomach churned. "Got it."

"And stay away from the main cabinet," Acid added. "It's wired to the alarm."

The knot in my chest tightened. I didn't want this. But I needed it. For Noah. Always for Noah.

Acid glanced at me once more before jerking his chin toward Butch. Without another word, they disappeared into the dark.

Razor was already moving toward the street. "Come on, slow coach," she tossed over her shoulder.

I fell in behind her, pushing back the dread sinking its claws deeper with every step.

She turned, her tone flat. "Back in a couple of hours. Don't be late. You know what happens if you are."

I nodded.

The night swallowed her whole.

And I kept walking, the weight of what came next pressing down like a storm.

Chapter 8
Willow

I barely had time to process it before I found myself in front of the jewelry store. Streetlights flickered on, casting jagged shadows across the pavement. The cold bit at my skin, but it was the tension in my chest that hurt the most.

One job: stand guard.

The thought spun in my head like a broken record, offering no comfort. I crossed my arms, shifting from foot to foot, eyes darting between darkened buildings and the rare passerby. I wasn't part of the big plan, but I still had a role. I had to make sure nothing went wrong.

Inside, the others moved with precision. Razor glided to her post, eyes sharp and calculating. Acid shot me a glance—arms folded, face unreadable.

"Willow. Stay here. Watch the front. Don't let anything slip past you."

I gave a sharp nod. No arguments. This wasn't my world, but I was in it now. And I had to survive.

Butch and Blaze were already prowling the display cases like predators. Butch moved quietly, efficient and steady. Blaze, eyes gleaming with adrenaline, hopped from case to case, barely containing her excitement.

"Don't touch the middle case," Acid warned, already turning toward the safe. "Alarm's wired to it."

A knot formed in my gut.

Then—sharp, piercing—the alarm exploded into the silence, slicing the air. My body locked up. Heart racing. Cold sweat broke across my skin.

"We triggered the alarm!" Acid's voice was tight, panicked. He whipped toward Razor. Her eyes mirrored his panic.

"What now?"

"There's a back exit," he snapped. "Move—everyone out the back!"

Sirens wailed in the distance, growing louder. Red and blue lights began to smear across the walls and sidewalk. My chest clenched.

"Quick, let's go!" Razor shouted, already running.

My legs took over before my mind could. I pushed through the store, lungs burning, heart pounding. I slammed through the rear exit, bursting into the cold night air—

And stopped.

The alley was empty.

No voices. No footsteps. Just the low, fading hum of two trail bikes disappearing into the dark.

They left me.

Every one of them—Razor, Blaze, Acid, even Butch. Gone. Like I'd never been part of it. Like I was nothing.

I froze mid-step, breath catching in my throat. Sirens screamed closer. Panic crawled up my spine. My mouth opened before I could stop it.

"Razor!" My voice cracked. "Razor!"

Silence. Just the wind. Just shadows.

Then—boots on concrete. Heavy. Fast. Closing in.

Police.

I turned—too late. They were already there, uniforms flooding the alley from every side. A gun raised.

"Freeze! Drop to the ground!"

My knees buckled. I hit the pavement hard, arms up, hands trembling too violently to hold steady.

Cold metal snapped around my wrists. Tight. Final.

That sound—God, that sound.

It felt like a door slamming shut on the last piece of freedom I had.

I'm being arrested.

The words hit harder than the pavement. My breath left me. No tears. Just shock. Like I'd been hollowed out.

This wasn't supposed to happen. I wasn't even supposed to be in there.

Firm hands dragged me to the patrol car. Faces blank. I was just another problem to file away.

The back seat reeked of sweat and disinfectant. Cracked leather clung to my skin. A police radio buzzed above it all— cold, detached.

I stared out the window, throat dry.

Where does this end?

How much worse can it get?

Will anyone even care I'm gone?

I had no answers.

Just silence.

Just me.

And a world that was already moving on without me.

Chapter 9
Willow

The overhead lights buzzed—white, blinding—like they were trying to burn through my skull. The longer I sat, the heavier the air grew, thick and suffocating, clinging to my skin like guilt.

I shifted, restless in the hard metal chair, every position more unbearable than the last. My throat felt dry—dusty, cracked—like I'd swallowed regret and couldn't wash it down. A lump sat lodged in my chest, immovable.

Sweat trickled down my spine. I wiped my forehead quickly, hoping he hadn't noticed. Couldn't let him see me unravel.

Not yet.

The room felt hot. Too hot. Deliberately hot.

Was that part of the game?

I scanned the space, searching for something steady, something real to anchor me—but all I could feel, all I could see, was him.

Detective Pierce.

He moved like the air belonged to him. Calm, contained, and terrifying in his silence. The kind of man who didn't need to raise his voice to break someone.

He glanced my way.

That was all it took.

His eyes met mine, and everything else blurred—his voice drowned beneath the pounding of blood in my ears.

Boom. Boom. Boom.

Too fast. Too loud.

It felt like my heart was trying to claw its way out of my chest.

I gripped the edges of the chair, knuckles burning. Muscles screaming to curl in, to vanish under his gaze. But I sat stiff, pretending not to drown. Pretending he hadn't already peeled me open.

Those sharp blue eyes didn't just look at you. They saw. They stripped.

And I knew—he wasn't asking questions.

He was watching me splinter.

"From what I hear," he said at last, his voice low, coaxing, "you've been up to no good."

I nodded once, stiff, like even that small motion might shatter something. Sweat dripped from my brow, but I didn't move to wipe it again. I couldn't. Not under that gaze.

My breath came in shallow gasps. Every inhale scraped. Every exhale trembled.

Don't let him see it. Don't let him know you're breaking.

"Tell me," he said, tilting his head slightly, like he already knew the answer. "Who was with you?"

A beat.

Then, leaning in just enough to make my skin crawl—

"Was it a solo job, Willow?"

My mouth opened. Nothing came out. Dry air scraped my throat. I forced a swallow, forced the lie to crawl out.

"I was on my own."

The words hit the table like a paper bird. Fragile. Limp. Unconvincing.

I stared down, focused hard on a chipped corner in the wood. Anything to avoid his eyes.

But I felt it—his disbelief. Pressing down on me like a palm against my neck.

"You're telling me," he said slowly, stretching out every syllable, "you walked into the store, took all that jewelry, and made it out in under two minutes?"

Legs twitching under the table. Palms slick. My chest screamed for air. The room, the guilt, the heat—everything was closing in.

And he wasn't finished.

He leaned forward, hands planted on the table now, the space between us shrinking fast.

"So why didn't we find any of it on you?"

The question didn't just hang—it slapped.

My breath hitched. Somewhere between a sob and a scream.

He knew exactly where to press. Which thread to tug.

Because here's the truth—I didn't steal the jewelry.

But I knew who did.

And saying their names? That would be a death sentence.

I stayed quiet.

And prayed that silence wouldn't destroy me faster than the truth ever could.

Chapter 10
Willow

I felt sick—nauseous in a way that started deep in my stomach and clawed its way up my throat. My mind scrambled, searching for something—anything—to say. An excuse. A lie. A softened truth to survive.

But when I opened my mouth, nothing came out. My tongue stuck to the roof of my mouth. My throat was sandpaper. My voice, gone.

"You weren't alone," Detective Pierce said, no longer pretending to be gentle. There was weight behind his voice now—a sharper edge. "Who were you working with?"

I swallowed hard, the motion painful. My body locked tight, bracing for a blow I couldn't see. I couldn't tell him. I wouldn't.

They'd already left me—took off without looking back, like I was nothing, like I didn't matter. But still, I couldn't hand them over. Not like this. Not when the world already felt like betrayal waiting to happen.

My hands twitched in my lap. Muscles jittered with nerves I couldn't contain. I picked at the frayed edge of my sleeve—a nervous habit I'd picked up as a kid. It was the only thing grounding me, keeping me from unraveling right there in front of him.

I can't, I reminded myself. I can't give them up.

Detective Pierce's eyes narrowed. The shift was there—he was closing in, trying to corner me.

"Is it because it's family?" His voice was slow, deliberate, like he was dropping traps. "Your boyfriend?" He paused. "Or maybe a girlfriend." He leaned in closer. "Maybe a friend."

I flinched. Just slightly. He caught it. Of course, he did. He was watching me like a hawk watching something bleed.

Then he leaned in even closer, face inches from mine. His words cut through the thin veil of composure I had left.

"It's your friends who left you, isn't it?"

That word—friends—landed like a punch to the gut.

Friends don't leave you to take the fall. Friends don't disappear into the night while you're dragged into the back of a patrol car. Friends don't sit safe and quiet while you face a record.

But I still couldn't say their names.

Because whatever they were—friends, mistakes, survival— they were all I had.

And even now, shaking, cornered, breaking apart, I couldn't betray the only people who once made me feel less alone.

So I stared back at Detective Pierce, lips trembling, pulse pounding, and said nothing.

Because silence was all I had left.

I bit my lip hard, tasting blood. The guilt gnawed at me—not just gnawing anymore—it was tearing me apart from the inside, carving holes in whatever strength remained. My fingers moved on their own, pulling loose strands from my sleeve, one after another, just to keep my hands busy. To stop myself from falling apart.

They'd left me. Didn't come back for me. Not Razor. Not Blaze. Not even a glance over their shoulder.

And Barb? She hadn't bailed me out. Hadn't even called.

I was alone. I always had been.

Detective Pierce's voice cut through my thoughts, sharp and unrelenting. "You're scared of them, aren't you?"

Then his tone shifted—gentler, like he was pretending to care. But underneath that softness, there was something cold, calculated. "What scares you more, Willow? Going to prison… or them coming after you?"

A lump swelled in my throat—thick, suffocating. Not just fear—betrayal. The realization hit harder than anything else: They'd used me.

They let me stand out in the open while they slipped away through the cracks. They knew the risks. They knew. And they left me to rot while they walked free.

His words kept coming—low and steady, like knives.

"They left you behind, Willow. Slipped out the back and left you holding all the blame. You're the one who got caught. You're the one they sacrificed."

He leaned in quieter this time. Almost gentle. Almost.

"Tell us who your friends are… and we can help you. We can make a deal."

I couldn't breathe. My chest rose and fell in shallow, panicked gasps. The room tilted like the world was cracking open beneath me, and I was slipping straight into it.

The thought of prison twisted my stomach, bile rising. The idea of cooperating—selling them out—made it worse.

But his voice painted it—steel bars, hard beds, locked doors, no way out.

I wanted to run. To scream. To have someone care enough to get me out.

But there was nowhere to go. No one to care. I was trapped.

My mind spun. I never wanted this. I was only the lookout— eyes on the street, just in case. I didn't steal. Didn't hurt. But that didn't matter.

The girls—they knew exactly what they were using me for. They'd gotten away. I was the one sitting here. Handcuffed. Alone. Facing a future I never asked for.

I never wanted to do this in the first place.

But now? I'd already lost.

And I didn't know what was worse—what they did to me… or that I still couldn't bring myself to turn them in.

"Tell us what happened," Detective Pierce urged, his voice smooth now—coaxing like offering something precious instead of tightening a noose. "We can offer you a way out."

I hesitated. Every part of me screamed don't do it. Don't open your mouth. Don't betray what little I had left.

But my body was too tired to fight.

Too broken to carry the weight of loyalty to people who had proven I meant nothing.

"I..." My voice cracked, trembling so badly I barely recognized it. "What are you offering?"

Detective Pierce smiled—not kind, but the smile of a man who knows he has you cornered, bleeding, begging.

"Community service," he said like it was a gift. "How does that sound?"

My heart stumbled. Not prison. Not cold cells where walls close in tight enough to forget how to breathe. Community service—a chance to claw my way out.

I swallowed, the sharp edge of reality slicing through the fragile bubble of hope.

"What about protection?" I whispered, shame burning the back of my throat. "They'll kill me."

For the first time, something flickered across Detective Pierce's face—almost human.

"I can't offer witness protection," his voice quieter now, almost regretful. "Not for this crime. But if you help us… if you give us what we need… we can put them away for a long time."

My eyes dropped to the scuffed floor beneath me. The harsh fluorescent lights blurred my vision.

Fear gnawed—sharp, relentless.

If I didn't take this deal, I knew exactly what would happen.

If I did… I wasn't sure I'd survive it either.

"I'm not sure," I murmured, voice so small it barely filled the space between us.

"You have my word," he said, low and thick, false comfort heavy in his tone. "You're doing the right thing, Willow."

The words rang hollow—like every other lie I'd been fed.

But what choice did I have?

None. Absolutely none.

I lifted my chin, even as everything inside me crumbled, and nodded.

"Okay."

The word tasted like blood and regret.

The weight of the decision settled over me—a thick, suffocating blanket. Final.

As I opened my mouth to speak, to reveal the details I'd sworn to keep locked away, something inside me broke.

The worst part was I didn't even know there was anything left to break.

I thought I'd lost it all—hope, pride, trust, pieces of myself I'd never get back.

But this was deeper—a kind of ache without screams or tears. Just silence. Heavy. Suffocating.

It settled in my chest like grief. Like saying goodbye to something I hadn't realized I'd been holding onto.

A quiet, painful heartache blooming in the emptiest part of me.

I could only hope it would pass. That I wouldn't have to feel it again.

Because if I do… I don't know if I'll survive it. Not this time.

It was with that pain I realized no one was coming to save me.

No one ever had.

I had to look after myself because no one else would.

I'd been alone this whole damn time—loyal to people who wouldn't even slow down long enough to notice they'd left me bleeding.

Maybe it was time I started acting like it.

Maybe it was time I looked out for number one. For me.

Chapter 11
Willow

Sitting alone in the sterile confines of my cell, I had too much time to think. The days blurred into a haze of stale air, uncomfortable silences, and a parade of faces who looked like they had given up on the world — and on themselves — long ago.

Each morning began the same way: boots on concrete, the clinking of keys, and the low groan of the cell block waking up. Meals arrived, tasteless and lukewarm, dropped off by guards who never met my eyes. I sat on the edge of my cot, staring at the bars, my mind swinging between panic and resignation.

The cellblock was never quiet. Men and women shouted obscenities, their voices sharp and grating. Others sat in silence, their eyes hollow, as if they had nothing left to give. Then there were those who joked and laughed as if this was just another stop on their usual route. Watching them, I felt both out of place and dangerously close to becoming one of them.

But what stayed with me were the whispers — stories exchanged in low voices about who was guilty, who got off light, and who wouldn't be coming back. The weight of their crimes hung in the air, and with every new arrival, the walls seemed to close in tighter.

By the time the guards came for court, I'd made my decision: I was alone, as always. The world wasn't going to save me. It never had. And now, more than ever, I couldn't count on anyone else.

Chapter 12
Willow

The courtroom felt colder than my cell, with high ceilings stretching into nothingness. Footsteps echoed against the walls, blending with the low murmur of distant voices. I sat at the defendant's table, the polished wood cool beneath my hands.

I tried to keep still, but my fingers betrayed me, nervously picking at the frayed edge of my sleeve. The weight of what was to come pressed down like a storm. This wasn't just about what I'd done — it was about what I hadn't done, what I'd let happen to me, again and again.

My throat dried, aching as if every lie I'd ever been told was lodged there, choking me. No one was coming. No one would storm through that door and pull me out of this mess. No one would hold my hand or fight my battles or save me from the wreckage of everything I'd been through.

If I wanted out, if I wanted more, I had to claw my way up from the dirt. Me. Not Razor. Not Blaze. Not Barb. Not even the system pretending to offer second chances. Just me.

For the first time in what felt like forever, I stopped drowning in self-pity. I stopped replaying betrayals and pain like a broken record. Something new sparked inside me — quiet but sharp. Determination.

It wasn't loud or roaring. But it was real. And it burned hot enough to keep me from falling apart.

Maybe I'd been alone my whole life. But that didn't mean I had to stay broken. Not anymore.

Lost in thought, I barely noticed the warm hand on my shoulder until its steady pressure brought me back. My first instinct was to flinch, but something about it stopped me. It wasn't invasive or intimidating — it was reassuring.

I looked up to meet the eyes of a tall man, 6 foot 3, with an easy, open face framed by dark, neat hair. His sharp suit contrasted with the softness in his expression and the faint lines around his large brown eyes, as if he spent most of his time smiling. His quiet confidence felt foreign in the chaos of my life.

"Hey, Willow," he said with warmth that seemed to stretch time itself. "I'm Finn Saunders. Your public defender. I'll be representing you today. Nice to meet you."

His hand was still extended. For a moment, I just stared, my mind scrambling. No one had ever said that to me with genuine warmth. He knew what I'd done — he had to — and yet there was no judgment in his voice or steady gaze. How?

Startled, I reached out and gave a weak, awkward shake. "Uh... nice to meet you too," I muttered, barely above a whisper, cheeks burning as I looked away.

He smiled, understanding and unforced. "I've discussed the deal with Detective Pierce," he explained calmly. "We're all on the same page. You're going to be okay, Willow."

Okay. The word echoed in my mind like a distant promise. How could I be okay after everything? After this?

Finn didn't push for a response. Instead, he sat beside me, arranging papers with quiet efficiency. I turned back toward the judge's table, thoughts still spinning. His words clung to me, but belief was hard to find.

The courtroom fell silent as the bailiff ordered everyone to rise. I stood automatically, the clinking of chains loud in the quiet room. Finn nodded briefly, reassuring, but I couldn't shake the feeling that everything was about to spiral.

The judge appeared, towering on his elevated bench, his gaze neutral but heavy. His scrutiny pressed against my chest like a stone.

"You may sit," he said.

I sank back into the cold wooden chair, tension settling between us.

"Willow," the judge continued, "I understand you've made a deal with Detective Pierce. You've provided information leading to arrests in exchange for community service."

I wiped sweat from my forehead, unable to meet his eyes. I focused on the rough table, grounding myself. Finn glanced at me, waiting.

"Speak up, Willow."

"Yes, Judge," I whispered.

He studied my case file, then the foster care documents. "I've reviewed your history. I don't believe you have bad intentions, but you need help. I'm sentencing you to five hundred hours of community service, with additional conditions."

My breath caught.

"Court-mandated therapy," he said, piercing through me. "Your upbringing was difficult. I want to give you every chance to turn things around."

I shifted, unsure, but knew I had no choice.

"And your school expulsions were mostly due to association, not direct violations. Wrong place, wrong people," he said, softer now.

Guilt pricked at me, recalling all the times I'd just tried to survive.

"You'll also attend the troubled teens program at the community college and finish your high school certificate. It's not too late."

I wanted to protest, but the words stuck. I nodded meekly.

"Do you think you can abide by these terms?"

Finn gave a small nod. I looked back at the judge and slowly said, "Yes, Judge."

He looked down, unreadable. "Then jail time won't be necessary. But turn your life around, Willow. Don't let me see you here again. I won't be so lenient next time."

My heart raced. A chance — slim but real.

"Court is adjourned."

Relief mixed with bitter reality. Community service, therapy, college — all reminders of how far I'd fallen and how much I had left to rebuild.

The courtroom emptied until only Finn and I remained. He leaned close. "You're doing the right thing. This is your chance. Don't waste it."

I nodded, unsure if I was ready. The judge had given me a chance, but I felt like I was standing on the edge of something too big to face.

As we walked out, my footsteps echoed in my mind, the cold weight of my sentence settling in. This was my life now — one step at a time.

Chapter 13
Willow

I shifted uncomfortably in the hard plastic chair, the chill of the police station creeping into my skin like an unwelcome guest. The fluorescent lights overhead buzzed faintly, casting a stark, sterile glow over dull grey walls. The air held a strange cocktail of stale coffee, sugary doughnuts, and the sharp tang of industrial disinfectant—a sensory assault that deepened the unease coiling in my chest.

My fingers picked at the threadbare sleeve of my jacket. Every sound seemed amplified: the distant clatter of keyboards, muffled voices behind closed doors, the rhythmic squeak of a chair. My throat felt dry, but I couldn't ask for water. This place wasn't new to me, but familiarity did nothing to ease the tightening knot inside.

Detective Pierce leaned casually against his desk. His unbuttoned jacket hung loose over a neatly pressed shirt. Though his stance was relaxed, his eyes scanned the room with quiet intensity. When he smiled, it was measured—neither warm nor cold—walking a line between empathy and authority, leaving me unsure whether I was comforted or cornered.

"You're free to go, Willow." His voice was even but firm.

I nodded, swallowing hard. My palms were clammy despite the chill. "Just stay out of trouble, and you'll be fine," he added, softening. His eyes carried a glimmer of hope. "No more running with anyone who could drag you back."

The words slipped out before I could stop them, bitter and raw. "Razor, Blaze…" I barely whispered, my thoughts spiraling before I could finish.

"They're locked up." His voice cut through my spiraling fears with calm finality. A quiet reassurance: the shadows I feared were caged, at least for now. It didn't erase the scars, but it was something.

"You're not all bad, Willow." His words hung heavy in the air. I looked up, startled. After so many judgments, hearing something hopeful felt like stepping into sunlight after years in darkness.

Before I could respond, he straightened and slid a thin file toward me. "Make sure you give this a shot. It's your last chance."

The file felt heavier than it looked. Therapy. Community service. College. A roadmap to redemption, if I could find the courage to follow it.

I took a shaky breath, voice steadier than I felt. "Yes, Detective."

His expression hardened, seriousness replacing warmth. "If you get caught and end up back in court, there won't be any deals left to save you from jail."

The weight of his words settled like a shroud. I swallowed hard, images of a courtroom and a falling gavel flashing behind my eyes.

His tone softened again. "The details are in there — therapist, community service, college, probation. You've got five days to get started."

I nodded, unable to trust my voice. The file felt foreign, like a lifeline I wasn't sure I deserved.

Detective Pierce studied me, searching for a sign of resolve. Finally, a faint, almost hopeful smile. "Hope I don't see you again, Willow."

A small, tentative smile tugged at my lips. "Me too."

The hum of the lights filled the silence as I stood, legs unsteady but determined. I gripped the file tightly, as if the papers inside could keep me grounded. Each step toward the door was a march away from the life I was leaving behind.

At the threshold, I glanced back. Detective Pierce was already flipping through another case, not looking up.

With a quiet exhale, I stepped into the hallway. The cool air hit like a wave — relief and unease washing over me. Freedom, I reminded myself, came with fragile conditions. His words echoed: *Just stay out of trouble.*

The door clicked shut behind me, reverberating through the quiet corridor as I walked away. My jacket clung tightly, a small comfort against the unknown. Outside, the morning stretched vast and indifferent — the future waiting, demanding: therapy, community service, college, a shot at redemption.

Chapter 14
Willow

At home, the creak of old floorboards and cluttered remnants of my life greeted me like old companions. I paused in the doorway, eyes drifting over scattered clothes, leaning stacks of books, a faint layer of dust. This space wasn't just a makeshift home; it reflected everything I'd been holding onto, both good and bad.

I set the file on the table, its weight still heavy in my hands. Not just instructions — a roadmap pointing toward something I'd been running from for too long. A chance to be better. To start again.

But first, I needed to wash off the dirt and sweat clinging to me. In the bathroom, my reflection caught me off guard — eyes shadowed with exhaustion, lips pressed tight like I was bracing myself. Smudges beneath my eyes told the story of restless nights. Yet beneath it all, something else stared back: determination.

The hot water and steam washed over me, loosening the tension knotted in my shoulders, eroding the grip of old fears. The cleanse wasn't just physical. It was symbolic — a small act signaling the end of one chapter and the start of another.

Stepping out, steam clinging to the air, I caught my reflection again. This time I saw someone ready — not perfect, but ready to try.

The resolve sparked like dry kindling catching flame. I couldn't wait for tomorrow. Starting my new life had to begin today.

Back in my bedroom, I opened the file carefully. Therapist, community service, college, probation — daunting, but I wouldn't let that stop me.

I grabbed my phone, fingers hesitated briefly before pressing call. Each ring felt like a step forward — a promise I was done running.

When the receptionist answered, I took a steady breath. "Hi, this is Willow. I'd like to schedule an appointment."

The words felt strange, like new clothes, but right. This was the first step — and there would be many more.

The future loomed uncertain, but I wasn't afraid anymore. Today was the day I chose to stop looking back and start moving forward.

Chapter 15
Willow

When I stepped into the kitchen, the comforting hum of the fridge and the soft glow of the overhead light greeted me. Noah's face lit up the moment he saw me, his smile wide and unreserved—such a stark contrast to the weariness weighing on me. His enthusiasm was infectious, a bright reminder of why I had to keep pushing forward.

"Willow!" he called, his voice high and jubilant as he darted toward me. Before I could brace myself, he wrapped his arms around my waist, pressing his cheek into my stomach.

"I missed you," he murmured, words muffled but warm against me.

"I missed you too, buddy." I hugged him tightly. The familiar scent of basketball rubber and faint sweat clung to him. My chest ached—love for this little boy who believed in me so wholeheartedly, and guilt for the times I'd let him down.

Noah pulled back just enough to look up at me, his freckled face glowing with innocent excitement. "Can we have pancakes every day now?" Hope filled his eyes, almost painful in its intensity.

I chuckled softly, shaking my head. Crouching to his level, I brushed a stray lock of his dirty orange hair from his face. "Sorry, buddy. The job didn't work out. But I'm working on it. We'll be okay."

His eyes searched mine, as if seeking confirmation I wasn't just saying empty words. I smiled reassuringly and ruffled his hair—more for me than him.

"I'm going out today to take care of some stuff. You be good, alright?"

He nodded solemnly, then grinned, lighting up the darkest corners of my heart. "Okay, Wills."

As I stood, his small hand lingered in mine before he let go, running off to whatever game he'd been playing before I arrived.

Leaning on the kitchen table, the weight of everything pressed down—Noah's trust, the therapy appointment, the promise of a better life. But for the first time in a long while, it didn't feel suffocating. It felt like a reason to fight.

I straightened and took a steadying breath. Noah deserved pancakes every day, and so much more. Starting today, I was going to do everything I could to make sure he got it.

Chapter 16
Willow

The therapy office waiting room felt sterile—almost too perfect. Neutral tones, meticulously arranged chairs, and a faint scent of lemon cleaner created an orderly but unwelcoming space. I tapped my foot restlessly, breaking the unnerving silence. Therapy. Of all the things I had to endure to stay out of jail, this felt the most surreal.

The door opened with a soft click. A man stepped out—Blake, the therapist, I was told. Younger than I expected, maybe mid-twenties, tall, 6 foot, with sharp, clean-cut features. His hair was perfectly styled, and his navy-blue tie sat straight against a crisp white shirt. He carried himself with easy confidence, a tablet in one hand and a sleek black notebook in the other.

"Willow?" His voice was warm and inviting, a sharp contrast to the cold order of the room.

I stood reluctantly, the weight of his gaze making me feel seen in a way that was uncomfortable. He smiled—not forced or professional, but genuine, as if glad to meet me.

"Thanks for waiting. Sorry I'm late." He motioned for me to follow. "I'm Blake. Come on in."

The office was just as clean and organized as the waiting room, but with a deliberate warmth. Bookshelves lined one wall, the books well-read, a few open notebooks tucked between them. A polished wooden desk stood in the corner, nearly bare except for a neatly stacked folder and a framed photo. The soft scent of wood mixed with faint coffee aroma from a sleek machine on a side table.

"Make yourself comfortable," Blake said, gesturing to the couch. He settled into the chair across from me, his movements deliberate but relaxed—like he wanted me to know he was paying attention without judgment.

"You weren't expecting me, were you?" he asked, breaking the silence with a playful smile.

I tilted my head, masking unease with oblivion. "Don't know what you mean." But I knew exactly.

"Most people picture an older guy," he said, leaning back just enough to seem approachable. "Glasses, grey hair, maybe a sweater vest. I'm 25—sorry to disappoint."

Caught off guard by his honesty, I shrugged. "Maybe I was."

His laugh was soft and genuine, amused but not mocking. "It's okay. I get that a lot. If it helps, I think I'm better at this than a guy in a sweater vest would be."

I tried not to smile but failed, feeling the corners of my lips lift. There was something disarming about the way he carried himself—warm but not overbearing, professional without being cold.

He leaned forward slightly, resting his forearms on his knees. "Let me guess. People see you and think troublemaker. Clutch their bags tighter, cross the street when they see you coming. Maybe even whisper as you walk by."

My stomach twisted. He was too close to the truth, words pulling at wounds I hadn't realized were so raw. I folded my arms defensively. "Close enough. But don't act like you didn't think the same when you saw me."

Blake shook his head, his expression softening. "Honestly? I saw a pretty lady with pink hair, bright, beautiful, curious blue eyes."

Did he just say pretty? Beautiful eyes? My chest tightened and my hands clammed up. No one had ever described me that way. Before I could think of a sarcastic response, he continued.

"A timid lady who looked like she's carrying the weight of the world on her shoulders. And I wondered why she thought she had to do it all alone."

I forced a laugh, hollow. "Timid? That's a first."

"Not timid," he corrected. "Tough. But I think there's more to you than that. I want to get to know that part."

I looked away, the vulnerability stirring inside me making me uncomfortable. "Everything you need to know is in my file." I wanted to shut the door on the conversation before it went any deeper.

"I haven't read it," he replied calmly. "Files tell me facts. I want to know who you are, not just what you've been through."

His response threw me. Most people used my file as a cheat sheet to judge me. But Blake didn't. It left me feeling raw—like a mirror held up to parts of myself I didn't want to see.

"Let's just stick to the basics," I said, trying to steer us back to safer territory.

Blake didn't push. Instead, he asked small, surprising questions—why I dyed my hair pink, my favorite childhood song. His curiosity felt genuine, unnerving in its honesty.

When the session ended, he stood, smoothing a non-existent wrinkle from his shirt before offering an easy smile. "I'd like to see you again tomorrow. I usually meet new clients daily for the first couple of weeks. How does that sound?"

I hesitated, the weight of his offer pressing against my instincts to run. Against better judgment, I nodded. "Sure."

"Great." He walked me to the door. His hand brushed lightly against my back as I stepped out—a gesture so brief and natural it almost felt like reassurance.

"See you tomorrow, Willow."

As I walked out into the cool air, I tried to shake the unfamiliar feeling creeping up my spine. He's just doing his job, I told myself. But the quiet, persistent voice in the back of my mind whispered something different: *What if he really does care?*

Chapter 17
Blake

The door clicked shut behind her, and for a moment, I sat in stillness. The scent of worn leather and rain lingered faintly in the room, but it was the memory of her eyes—guarded, impossibly blue—that stayed with me most.

I opened the fresh new, leather bound journal that I had yet to fill with notes about her, fingers grasping the pen as it hovered over the first page, took a moment and then began writing the session notes while the interaction was still fresh.

Session #1

I arrived approximately four minutes late to the appointment due to a delayed intake call with another client. Willow showed no signs of agitation or frustration due to my lateness. In fact, she appeared entirely unbothered—legs crossed, slouched low in the chair, a faint smirk on her face as though she'd been expecting me to disappoint her.

As I closed the door, I made a light remark about her probably expecting someone older, maybe glasses, grey hair, in a sweater vest. She cracked a dry smile, called it "Maybe." I said I preferred to think I was better than that. The joke gave me a segue—to explore how people might judge her on appearance alone, and I offered her a few honest observations. That she seemed sharper than she let on.

That there was more beneath the surface. Her response was predictably sarcastic.

Her body stiffened—arms folded, eyes narrowed. A shift in her posture I've come to associate with defence. Vulnerability, shut down.

I probed, gently. Asked about who she is, not what she's done.

Every time I got close to peeling back a layer, she changed the subject or steered the conversation to safer ground. She tolerated basic questions—favourite music, why her hair's pink, what she'd eat if she could choose anything—but anything deeper was met with evasion.

She struggles to accept even mild praise. I paid her a compliment, deliberately—calm, simple, sincere—and watched her shrink from it. Not with words, but posture. As if kindness was a spotlight she didn't want.

I deliberately avoided reading her foster file beforehand.

I told her as much. I wanted to meet her without the bias of someone else's version of her life.

That seemed to surprise her. Her shoulders lowered slightly. Her tone softened for a moment. A small but notable shift in rapport.

I paused, tapping the pen on the desk gently

before continuing.

By the end of the session, I sensed a reluctant willingness to return. No promises. But less resistance.

That was enough.

As she moved to leave, I stood. Our eyes met. Something in the air shifted—something I couldn't quite name. I walked her to the door, polite, professional. But in those last steps, my hand—

without thought, without intention—brushed against the small of her back. Light. Barely there.

She froze, just for a second.

I felt the tension coil in her shoulders. But she didn't flinch. Didn't step away. She let it happen.

I shouldn't have done it. It was unnecessary.

A line crossed, even if imperceptibly.

I leaned back in my chair, exhaling slowly.

There's something about her. A gravity. And despite every measure of training, discipline, and control—I felt it.

I'm not sure what that means yet.

But I'll need to be careful. Very careful.

Therapeutic recommendations:

Continue light, rapport-building conversation. Begin exploring client's current support network and environment without pushing for trauma disclosure. Monitor comfort levels closely. Avoid all physical contact.

Chapter 18
Willow

The room was silent, broken only by the faint whir of the fan in the corner. Its steady hum filled the stillness, itng I lay sprawled on the bed, staring at the ceiling where shadows from the streetlight outside flickered like restless ghosts. The air in my tiny bedroom felt dense, heavy with my swirling thoughts.

Fragments of the day replayed in my mind, jagged and disjointed, like an old film reel stuck on repeat. I'd walked into therapy expecting something clinical—cold questions, calculated judgments, a stranger peeling back layers of my life like a puzzle to solve. Instead, I got Blake.

Even his name stirred something tight and unfamiliar in my chest. Not cold. Not clinical. His gaze was steady, kind even, filled with something I couldn't quite name. Understanding? Curiosity? Whatever it was, it wasn't pity. Never pity.

I traced the edge of the pillow, trying to anchor my thoughts. His words echoed uninvited: Pretty. Beautiful eyes. The memory of his voice warmed my neck—a heat I quickly shoved aside. He probably says that to everyone, I told myself. It didn't mean anything. Yet, stubbornly, those words nestled into a corner of my mind.

I rolled onto my side as a slow exhale escaped me. Blake was different. Genuine. He hadn't treated me like a problem to fix or a lost cause to discard. It was disarming, this kind of attention. People didn't look at me like I mattered.

And that was the most terrifying part—the possibility that maybe, just maybe, he really did see something in me.

No. I squeezed my eyes shut, as if shutting out the thought might help. Don't be stupid, Willow. He's just doing his job. He has to act like he cares. But if that was true, why did it feel like he meant it?"

But even as I tried to convince myself, the memory of his smile tugged at my mind. The way his eyes softened when they met mine, as though he wasn't just going through the motions— like he genuinely wanted to understand me. That kind of attention felt dangerous. Like standing at the edge of a cliff and leaning too far forward.

A yawn broke through my thoughts. I pressed a hand to my mouth, suddenly aware of the exhaustion pulling at my limbs. The past few days had worn me down—the sleepless nights in that freezing jail cell, the endless hours bracing myself for judgment. Yet now, in the quiet solitude of my room, it all felt heavier, as though the walls themselves were closing in.

The red glow of the digital clock on the nightstand caught my eye, its numbers blurring as I blinked against the dim light. There were still a few hours before Brandy and Summer would come crashing in with their chaos. For now, at least, I had a sliver of peace.

I pulled the blanket tighter around my shoulders, seeking a warmth the room couldn't provide. Tomorrow loomed—a therapy session with Blake. The thought stirred a mix of dread and curiosity. He wanted to see me every day for a while. I couldn't decide if that made me want to run or stay.

He wasn't like anyone I'd met. He didn't demand explanations I wasn't ready to give or push me into corners I couldn't escape.

As sleep crept in, the memory of his hand on my back surfaced—light, brief, but enough to leave an impression I couldn't shake. Not like the rough, selfish touches I'd learned to brace against. Something else entirely. Reassuring. Kind. Unsettling in a way I couldn't explain.

The darkness deepened, the mechanical whir a lullaby I couldn't quite surrender to. But even as I drifted toward sleep, Blake lingered in my thoughts—his voice, his smile, the way he looked at me, not like a problem to solve, but someone who mattered.

Chapter 19
Willow

I pushed open Blake's office door. The familiar scent of coffee and warm wood greeted me, just like last time. Sunlight streamed through the large window, casting soft patterns across the carpet. Blake wasn't at his desk; he stood by the door, his smile warm and inviting.

"Good morning, Willow." His voice carried the same ease and calm that unsettled me yesterday.

I hesitated in the doorway, awkwardness settling like a heavy cloak. Blake looked so at home here. I felt like an intruder in a world too pristine for someone like me.

"Morning," I muttered, eyes flickering to the floor before meeting his.

He smiled wider and reached toward his desk. "I saw this yesterday and thought of you."

He held out a small pink notebook, its bright cover vivid against the muted tones of his office. I stared, unsure how to respond to such a simple, unexpected gesture.

"A notebook?" My voice wavered between skepticism and curiosity.

He nodded. "Thought you might like a place to jot down thoughts, songs, dreams... whatever's on your mind."

The notebook felt strange in my hands, its smooth cover foreign. Someone had gone out of their way for me. Unnerving. My fingers traced the edges, searching for grounding.

"Thanks." Quiet, but genuine.

Blake gestured toward the couch. "Take a seat. Let's get started."

I sank into the plush couch, still clutching the notebook. Its weight felt heavier than it should, as if carrying more meaning than he intended. Across from me, Blake settled into his chair, relaxed yet attentive, radiating easy confidence.

"What would you like to do today?" His look was open, unpressured. "It's entirely up to you."

The question caught me off guard. Part of me wanted to shrug it off, let him decide—it would

be easier. But something in the way he left it to me made me pause.

"Maybe we can just sit?" I mumbled shyly.

"Works for me." He leaned back, picking up a book from the table. "Mind if I read while you think?"

I shook my head, unsure what I was supposed to be thinking about.

Silence settled softly between us, filling the space like a gentle rhythm. Still, I couldn't relax. My fingers fidgeted with the notebook's cover, caught on the simple kindness of receiving it. I couldn't remember the last time someone gave me something for no reason.

Restless, I shifted, eyes wandering. Blake was absorbed in his book, calm and focused. My gaze landed on his desk—

everything radiated control, pens perfectly aligned, files stacked neatly, the surface spotless. So orderly. So Blake.

Then, in the corner, a photo caught my eye.

Before I realized it, I was standing beside the desk, drawn to the picture of a dark-haired woman, vibrant and smiling brightly.

"Is this your girlfriend?" The question slipped out.

Blake glanced up, amused but kind. "No." He set the book aside. "That's my sister."

"Your sister?"

He nodded. "We're close. Always have been."

"Why keep her picture here?" Curiosity tangled with something deeper.

He motioned for me to sit. I returned to the couch, clutching the notebook, waiting.

"Our parents weren't very involved. It was just the two of us growing up. We looked out for each other."

His words held a quiet vulnerability, foreign yet familiar.

"That's nice," I said, feeling my words fall short.

His gaze softened. "You don't have family?"

The question hit harder than I expected, pressing against an ache I thought I'd buried.

"Nope." Barely a whisper.

"Do you ever wish you did?"

"Nope," I said flatly, hoping to end it.

He leaned forward, elbows on knees. "That's a tough way to live."

I shrugged, grip tightening on the notebook. "You can't miss what you've never had."

Looking away, I added, "It doesn't bother me." The words rang hollow, even to me.

Stillness deepened, but he didn't press. Instead, a soft smile offered quiet reassurance.

"You're a smart young woman." His voice broke the silence.

"What?"

"It's true." His smile widened just enough to feel genuine. "I meant it yesterday, and I'll say it again."

Heat crept up my cheeks. I looked down, unsure how to respond.

"Thanks."

The session continued with gentle questions and quiet reassurances. When it ended, Blake rose.

"If you ever need to talk, you can reach me." He pulled out his phone, scrolling. "I put my number in the notebook. Call or text anytime."

I nodded, holding the notebook tighter. "Maybe." I knew it was an empty promise, but his tone made me want to believe.

He paused, thoughtful. "You have community service after this?"

I sighed, nodding.

"That's a big deal, Willow." Softness laced his voice. "Text me afterward. Tell me how it went, how you felt."

I hesitated, grip tightening. "Maybe."

His smile returned, steady and warm. "Hopefully, I can get you to trust me soon. I'm here to help." His eyes met mine with quiet determination.

His words lingered as I looked away, the intensity of his kindness making me feel both seen and exposed.

"Well," I said quickly, breaking the silence. "I better get going. Don't want to be late."

Blake nodded, stepping toward the door. "I'll show you out."

As I left, the faint brush of his hand against mine lingered like a spark beneath my skin. Not just a touch—warmth, alive, spreading up my arm and settling deep in my chest where nothing else stayed. The spot where our hands met tingled, as if the moment marked me.

I told myself it was nothing. An accident. He didn't mean it. But part of me—the part that still believes in something gentle— clung to it.

It felt like something was blooming inside me, something I didn't ask for, something I wasn't sure I could survive.

Chapter 20
Blake

The door clicks shut behind her.

Silence settles like dust—quiet, weighty, persistent. I let it linger, inhaling the space she leaves behind. The tension doesn't exit with her. It hangs, almost tangible, in the air.

I reach for her file.

The leather-bound journal creaks open. The pen hovers, then stalls.

Focus.

She sat across from me for fifty minutes. Same chair. Same crossed legs. Same jacket slipping off her shoulder like it always does—casual, unconscious, maddening. She rarely speaks, but when she does, it's deliberate. No filler. Every sentence carefully rationed, as though each one costs her more than she's willing to admit.

Session #2

Client arrived slightly late. No apology. Verbal engagement limited but intentional.

Exhibited continued hypervigilance: self-soothing behavior (plucking her sleeve), guarded posture, eyes scanning exits early in the session.

I pause.

However...

She held my gaze longer today.

When our hands brushed—briefly—as I guided her out, she didn't flinch. Didn't pull away. I should call it an accident. But it wasn't. There was a pull, subtle and undeniable.

I lingered, just enough to feel it. Just enough to wonder.

Her restraint is magnetic. It wraps around her like armor—delicate, worn thin at the edges, but still holding.

She's constantly on the verge of shattering, and yet she never breaks. That kind of strength... it's rare.

It's infuriating. It's irresistible.

I lean back, pen idle, fingers grazing my jaw.

She smelled like smoke again. Smoke and

something else—something soft, sweet, and lingering. It clings to the room, to my thoughts, long after she's gone.

This reaction I keep pretending is harmless? It's not. It's not just her beauty, though it's impossible to ignore. It's how she carries pain—not drowning in it, but mastering it.

Her silence doesn't feel like distance. It feels like resistance. Like defiance. And I want to know what's beneath it.

I shouldn't notice the curve of her mouth when she bites the inside of her cheek. Shouldn't wonder what her voice sounds like unguarded.

Shouldn't want to trace the tension in her shoulders with anything other than clinical detachment

But I do.

And that want—this pull—it's not normal. Not professional. And nothing I've felt with anyone else. Not this fast. Not this deep. Not like her.

She calls to the parts of me I bury under polished suits and perfect posture. The parts I don't let anyone touch.

She wouldn't bend. She'd push back. She might be the only person who ever could.

And that thought is dangerous.

I glance back at the file and finish the sentence.

Therapeutic recommendations:

Client beginning to show early signs of measured trust. Recommend maintaining current therapeutic pace. Boundaries remain essential.

I pause, then slowly close the file. Deliberate. Final.

Locking the drawer won't help.

She's already in places no file can reach.

Chapter 21
Willow

The sun hammered down on the community service administration building, its tall glass facade gleaming like a mirror under the relentless blue sky. A small crowd had gathered near the wide stone steps, the orange jumpsuits we wore blazing obnoxiously bright in the daylight—a not-so-subtle announcement of our status. I tugged at the stiff, synthetic fabric clinging to my skin, grimacing.

Frank, the coordinator, stood like a sentinel in front of us. Towering and broad-shouldered, his shaved head gleamed in the sun, and his light brown eyes scanned the group with unflinching precision. The wiry mix of white and brown in his beard hinted at years of grit and tolerance.

"I'm Frank," he barked. "I don't care why you're here. My job is to get your hours logged without anyone getting hurt. Got it?"

A scattered chorus of mumbled agreement followed.

"Today, you're cleaning up trash in the neighboring area. Work in pairs. No excuses. No complaints." He clapped his hands sharply. "Let's move."

Good. No room for drama. I stayed near the back as we trudged to the bus, keeping my head down.

The ride passed quietly, broken only by the bus's rattle and occasional murmurs. Outside, the city grew bleaker—graffiti walls, sagging buildings, the sour tang of stale grease in the air. When we arrived, Frank handed out gloves and trash bags with military precision, assigning partners.

I was tightening the knot on my bag when someone stepped into view. Tall, at least 6 foot 4, olive-skinned, long dark hair pulled into a messy bun, a crooked grin on his face. A full tattoo sleeve of snakes, tribal symbols, and red roses curled along his arm.

"Hey there, pretty lady. Looks like we're partners."

I ignored his outstretched hand, focusing on the knot.

"Not much of a talker, huh? That's okay. I don't bite. Unless you want me to."

A sharp glare from me earned a brief pause. Then his grin returned.

"You're gonna be a tough nut to crack. I like it."

Perfect. A flirt. Just what I needed.

I stepped away. He followed, unconcerned.

We worked in strained silence. Occasionally, he tossed out conversation starters, each one falling flat. As I bent to grab a crushed soda can, a shadow loomed. I straightened, heart thudding.

A man in the same jumpsuit stood too close. Shaved head, dark eyes, a malicious smirk.

"Willow, right?"

I froze.

"Razor sends a message," he murmured. "She's still pissed about what you did. Watch your back."

My stomach dropped.

"You stabbed her in the back," he hissed. "And when you least expect it, you'll get what's coming to you. Eye for an eye."

Before I could react, my annoying partner stepped in, his casual charm replaced with sharp steel.

"You're in the wrong section," he said, voice cold. "Back off."

The man sneered, raising his hands in mock surrender. "Just delivering a message." He shot me one last look. "You've been warned."

He walked off.

The shaking started immediately, hard and uncontrollable. My breath came fast and shallow, the world tilting beneath me. I couldn't anchor myself. Razor's threat echoed in my head like a scratched record, stuck on the ugliest part of the song.

"You okay?"

I looked up. He'd turned back, crouching slightly to meet my eyes.

I nodded, swallowing hard.

He studied me, then extended a hand. "I'm Braxton."

Reluctantly, I shook it. "Willow."

A playful grin touched his face. "She talks."

I almost smiled. Almost. But the danger still loomed too close.

"Looks like you've made an enemy," he said gently. "You sure you're all right?"

I didn't answer. What was I supposed to say? That Razor had minions and they whispered death threats in broad daylight? Sure. Totally fine.

I bent down, grabbing another piece of trash, trying to steady my hands.

"We've got a lot of hours ahead," he said. "I'd like to be friends."

I stood, giving him a pointed look. "Don't take this the wrong way, but I'm not interested."

He clutched his chest theatrically. "Brutal."

I sighed. "I just want to stay out of trouble. I've been given a second chance. I'm not wasting it."

Braxton nodded, a shadow passing through his gaze. "Fair enough. Who says I don't want the same thing?"

I shook my head and stepped away. "Nothing personal. I'd just rather be left alone."

"You're talking to me now. I like my chances."

I didn't respond. Just walked a little farther ahead, trying to put some distance between me and everything.

Including him.

Chapter 22
Braxton

The orange jumpsuit was a goddamn insult—scratchy, stiff, impossible to ignore, just like the sun beating down on us as we lined up in front of the community service building. But even in all that heat and noise, I saw her.

Pink hair pulled into a loose braid, strands falling free like she didn't care—or didn't have the energy to. Her head stayed low, shoulders curled in like armor. The others joked, postured, made noise. She was still. Like she didn't belong here. Like she was trying not to be seen.

But I saw her.

Not just her hair or the way she moved. It was everything. Sadness wrapped around her like a second skin, old and familiar. The kind that didn't start here—it had roots somewhere much deeper.

On the bus, I sat close without making it obvious. Leaned against the window, pretending not to look while I took in every detail. She stared outside, not tracking the streets or signs. Just… gone. Like her body was here, but her mind had retreated somewhere far off.

Up close, she was even more striking. Tanned skin, soft freckles scattered like stars across her nose. I caught myself counting them just to give my eyes something gentle to land on. Then her eyes—damn.

Blue. Not bright, not glittering. Deep. Like the whole ocean lived behind them. Calm, endless, and carrying sorrow too heavy to name. Eyes that once burned bright but had dimmed just to survive.

She didn't fidget or shift like the others. Just held herself in that quiet stillness. Like silence was the only place left that felt safe.

And I hated how much I understood that.

Frank—our overly cheerful overlord—started barking orders once we arrived. Splitting us into pairs. I made sure to be in her section before he could shuffle me off somewhere else.

She wasn't thrilled. Didn't even look at me when I offered a hand. Just focused on tying her bag like I didn't exist. I cracked a few harmless jokes. Her eyes flicked up, sharp and cutting. Cold enough to freeze fire.

Strangely, I liked it.

Not because she was playing hard to get. She wasn't. She just didn't want anyone in her space. The way she held that boundary—sharp, unwavering—spoke volumes. You only build walls that strong when someone's already broken in.

We picked up trash in silence. Awkward, yeah. But not tense. I gave her space, even if I couldn't stop watching her from the corner of my eye. Not in a weird way—just... drawn. Something in her mirrored something buried deep in me.

Then he showed up.

Big guy. Bad energy. Walked like he owned the place. I clocked him before she did. The second he stepped into her space, something in her changed. She froze. Her hand dropped what she was holding.

He leaned in, said something low. She flinched.

Didn't think—just moved. Stepped between them, voice low and cold enough to make him pause. He backed off, pretending it was nothing. But it wasn't.

When I turned back, she was shaking.

Not a surface tremble. This ran deeper, like her bones remembered something her lips wouldn't name.

"You okay?"

No answer. No eye contact. Then—barely—she nodded.

I offered my hand again. Not because she owed me anything. Just so she could choose.

This time, she took it.

"Willow," she murmured.

The name landed heavier than it should have. Soft. Quiet. Beautiful in a way that didn't ask to be noticed.

"She talks." I grinned.

A flicker—almost a smile.

I didn't push. Just worked beside her, letting the silence be whatever she needed it to be. After a while, she cracked the smallest window.

"I just want to stay out of trouble. I've been given a second chance. I'm not planning on wasting it."

That hit harder than I expected.

I liked that. I respected that.

Didn't say it. Just nodded, let her know I got it. I meant it. Whether she believed me or not didn't matter.

She told me she'd rather be left alone. Probably should've listened.

But I didn't.

Because I've seen what happens when people give up on each other. Watched too many sit in silence and rot in it. Maybe she didn't want saving—but she deserved not to be alone.

So, I stayed a step behind. Not in her way. Just... there.

Persistent. Quiet. Waiting.

Because sometimes, the ones who fight the hardest to be left alone are the ones hoping someone stays.

Chapter 23
Braxton

Willow moved with quiet determination, each bend to pick up trash more mechanical than the last. I watched her from a distance, trying not to make it obvious. She had the kind of presence that pulled you in—not because she was loud or flashy, but because she was holding something back. Whatever it was, it was buried deep, under layers of caution and control.

I couldn't stop thinking about that guy who'd confronted her. The way he loomed, the venom in his voice. That wasn't a spat—that was history. Dangerous history. She'd stood her ground, but the flicker of fear in her eyes was real. And for some reason, it made my chest tighten.

Frank's voice cut through the tension. "Good work, everyone. Head back to the bus."

I glanced at Willow. She gave Frank a polite nod, a tight smile that didn't reach her eyes. The kind of smile people wear when they've learned that showing nothing is safer than showing pain.

She started walking, head down. I crossed my arms, debating whether to follow. She wasn't the kind of girl who invited conversation. Hell, she looked like she'd bite the head off anyone who tried. But then there'd been that tiny moment—barely a second—when her eyes met mine and softened, just enough to make me wonder.

I caught up to her slowly. "So…" I rubbed the back of my neck, giving a sheepish grin. "Think I could get your number?"

She didn't stop walking. "Didn't you hear anything I said?"

"Yeah, I just thought… maybe carpooling to community service together would be more fun."

Her eyes rolled so hard I thought they might stick. "I'm happy walking."

She brushed past me. This time, I let her go.

Didn't mean I was giving up. She was different, and I'd always been drawn to complicated. Not the fake kind either. The real, sharp-edged, keep-your-distance kind. Like her.

"She's fascinating," I muttered to myself, leaning against a lamppost as the last of the sun slipped behind the trees.

The others boarded the bus. Through the foggy window, I found her again—curled up in her seat, closed off from the world. But I saw her. And I had a feeling she knew it.

She wasn't just another girl in an orange jumpsuit. There was a story buried in those guarded eyes. And maybe—just maybe—I'd get to hear it someday.

Chapter 24
Willow

I collapsed onto my bed, the thrum of the day still echoing in my bones. The room was quiet, too quiet. Even the fan humming in the corner couldn't drown out the noise in my head.

That threat kept replaying. *You stabbed her in the back. And when you least expect it, you'll get what's coming to you. Eye for an eye.*

I clenched the blanket. *She's in jail,* I reminded myself. *She can't touch me.*

But Razor had people. She always had people. That fear I'd buried crept back in like a slow leak.

The clock glowed in the dark—nearly midnight. I changed out of my jumpsuit, sliding into old pajamas that smelled like lavender and bleach. I crawled under the covers, hoping for sleep. It didn't come.

The sharp buzz of my phone made me jump. My heart did a weird stutter as I reached for it.

"I thought you were going to tell me how it went today?"

No name. Just the message.

"Who is this?" I typed back.

The reply came fast. "Oh, I'm a little hurt you've forgotten about me already. It's Blake."

My stomach twisted. Blake. I hadn't expected him to check in. Most people said things like that just to be polite.

"How did you get my number?"

"You made me go read through those stupid files to get it."

I winced. I didn't want him reading those. "Didn't think you were serious."

"Of course I was. So, how did the community service go?"

"It was fine." I hesitated, then added: "My partner was nice, but I'm not looking for friends."

"Everyone needs friends, Willow."

I stared at the screen, my fingers stalling. "I'm fine." Then, almost unwillingly: "There was this one guy…"

"Yes? What about him?"

Immediate regret.

"Never mind. Not your problem."

"If it's your problem, then it's my problem. We're working through things together now, remember?"

His words were reassuring and warm. Too warm.

I blinked hard, then typed, "I got threatened by someone I ratted on."

There. Said it.

"You have a session tomorrow. We'll talk then."

"I'm a rat. I deserve what I get." I threw the phone down before I could overthink it.

Buzz. Then again. And again.

I picked it up slowly.

"I'm sure that is not true."

"Willow?"

"You still there?"

Something twisted inside me.

"You might change your mind tomorrow… after you hear what I've done."

"Can't imagine I will. Till tomorrow. Night, Willow."

It was such a simple text. But somehow, it felt like an anchor.

"Night, Blake."

I placed the phone on the nightstand and curled deeper into the blankets.

He remembered. He actually remembered.

I wanted to believe him, trust that someone meant it this time. But the truth clawed at me: once people got too close, they always saw the same thing.

Nothing worth sticking around for.

Braxton crossed my mind. He'd been kind too—gentle, even. But that kind of guy? He always wanted something. They all did.

I wasn't giving anyone that chance again.

Still, as I drifted toward sleep, Blake's words stayed with me, echoing like a lullaby I wasn't sure I deserved.

Chapter 25
Willow

My hand hovered over the familiar door handle of Blake's therapy room. Hesitation swept through me like a cold wave. The strap of my bag bit into my shoulder as my stomach twisted. Was it nerves? Dread? Or the lingering weight of yesterday's chaos pressing down on my chest? I took a deep breath, trying to steady the tremor in my hands, then pushed the door open.

Blake stood across the room, impeccably dressed in his tailored suit. His professional mask softened by a warm, easy smile. Seeing him still made my heart race—like it was the first time, even though it wasn't.

"Morning, Willow." His voice was smooth, confident, carrying that strange mix of comfort and unease that always threw me off. He motioned for me to come in.

I nodded and stepped inside, fighting the tightness in my chest. "Morning," I muttered, barely above a whisper.

He gestured toward the couch, leaning on the back of his chair, eyes locked on me. "How are you feeling? Did you get some rest?"

I shrugged and lowered myself onto the cushions. The couch seemed to wrap around me, but it only made me more aware of the knot tightening inside. It was like the cushions wanted me to open up—something I wasn't sure I was ready to do.

"Okay, I guess," I admitted, voice small. "Still... a little worried."

Blake tilted his head, studying me with calm concern. "Tell me about it."

I bit my lip, twisting the hem of my sleeve. "I'm worried you'll see me differently," I blurted out.

His brow furrowed just a bit, voice steady. "I doubt that."

Shaking my head, I stared at my lap. "You're nice. Too nice. But you don't really know me. If I tell you everything…" My voice cracked. "You'll see I'm just a rat. A coward."

The words dropped like stones, heavy and cold. My eyes welled up before I could stop them, and my body shook with a sob I couldn't control.

"Hey." His chair creaked as he moved closer and knelt beside me. His voice was gentle but firm. "It's okay. Let it out."

His arms wrapped around me—strong, steady. My head rested on his chest, hearing the steady thump of his heart. His cologne—woody with a hint of citrus—wrapped around me. For a moment, it felt like safety, even if the situation was uncomfortable.

Embarrassment flushed through me, but I didn't pull away. For the first time in a long while, I let myself sink into the moment, allowed the calm to seep in.

His hold tightened slightly. "You don't need to hide it here. I'm here to help."

I pulled back, wiping damp cheeks, voice shaky. "Sorry. I shouldn't have done that."

Blake smiled gently. "How about we talk it through? No judgment."

I nodded, a mix of relief and dread swirling inside as I settled back into the cushions. He sat close beside me, and suddenly, the space between us felt too intimate.

"So," he leaned forward, thoughtful. "What feels comfortable to share?"

I hesitated, fingers picking at my sleeve. "I guess I should start with why I'm here. What brought me to this room, to you." He nodded, unreadable.

I swallowed hard. "It was a heist. Razor and Blaze planned it, with Acid and Butch. But something went wrong. The alarm went off... they ran." The memory stabbed sharp. "They left me. I got caught."

His eyes never left mine, steady and calm. "So you did what you had to do."

"They wouldn't protect me," I said bitterly. "I had to look out for myself. That's why I turned on them. Wanted a fresh start. Didn't want to be their pawn anymore."

Blake shifted, his hand brushing my leg—just a second, barely there—but it stole my breath. I froze, heart pounding. Was it deliberate? I didn't dare meet his eyes.

"That's it," I whispered. "That's who I am."

Silence fell. I exhaled slowly.

Blake leaned back, thoughtful. "Wow."

"I know." My voice stumbled over itself. "I'm terrible. I shouldn't have ratted them out. I'm a coward who couldn't face jail."

His voice was firm. "You're incredibly strong. Standing up for yourself. Protecting your future. That takes courage."

I looked away, throat tightening. "Doesn't feel like courage."

"Sometimes courage just feels like survival." He smiled softly.

His words settled heavy inside me. "Do you want to talk about how you got involved with them?"

Chapter 26
Willow

I nodded. "We met by chance. They saw how useful I could be. And I needed protection."

"Useful?" Blake asked carefully.

"They'd ask me to do things," I struggled, not wanting to be fully seen. "Things they thought were beneath them or too risky. A trade-off. Protection for favors."

His face didn't change, but his gaze weighed on me. "What kind of things?"

I hesitated, swallowing memories that clawed at me. "I'll explain," I said, voice tight.

Blake waited patiently, brow furrowed at my unease. He noticed everything—the way my fingers twisted my shirt's frayed sleeve, the tightness in my chest.

"You want to know how I got involved with Razor and Blaze?" My voice softened, reluctant. "It's not a story that'll make you think better of me."

He didn't flinch, just nodded, warm and patient, ready to listen.

"It started at school." My gaze dropped to my lap. "I was just trying to get through the day, keep my head down. But trouble… it always finds you when you least expect it."

I closed my eyes, letting the memory unfold.

The hallway buzzed with noise—students chattering, lockers slamming. Britany stood in the middle, her voice cutting through like a spotlight. She thrived on confrontation. Today, Raven was the target, clutching her coffee like a lifeline.

"You got it all over me!" Britany snapped, brushing at her jacket angrily.

Raven's face drained of color. "Oh my gosh, I'm so sorry."

"Watch where you're going," Britany sneered. "You think you're better than me? Just because you're carrying coffee like you're important?"

I lingered near the lockers, torn. The instinct to stay invisible wrestled with the urge to step in, to stop the cruelty.

Britany's voice rose. "So, this is my fault, huh?"

"No! I wasn't," Raven stammered.

"Good," Britany snapped, arms crossed. "Because I don't take kindly to baseless accusations."

My heart hammered. Any other day, it could've been me.

I nodded to myself and took a step forward—to help. But a voice stopped me cold.

"Hey, you."

The hallway fell silent. Razor stood there—confident, cold, dangerous. She leaned against the locker, hazel eyes locked on me. Blaze smirked beside her, arms crossed.

I froze. The crowd scattered, the argument ending abruptly.

Their presence pressed on me, paralyzing. Razor straightened slowly, deliberate. "Where do you think you're going?"

"I don't want trouble," I stuttered, stepping back.

A smirk curved her lips. "You already found it."

Blaze stepped forward, syrupy sweet. "Razor saw what you did earlier. You're not sneaky enough to go unnoticed."

My stomach dropped. I hadn't thought anyone saw me slip that candy bar from the vending machine. It wasn't something I did often—just when desperate. Razor had noticed. And she wasn't letting it go.

"I'll give it back," I blurted.

Razor laughed, low and humorless. "Why? You've got skills, Willow. Why waste them?"

"I don't do it often," I trembled. "Only when I need food."

She studied me, that unsettling gaze making my skin crawl. "Get used to it. Those skills need to be… harnessed."

Her voice dropped to a whisper. "You scratch my back, I'll scratch yours. Help me, and no one bothers you. Everyone will know you're one of my girls."

Blaze's smirk turned predatory. Razor's words suffocated me. I wanted to say no, to walk away, but Britany's taunts echoed, and the fear of being targeted again froze me.

"I don't know," I whispered.

Razor's smile vanished, replaced by a cold edge. "Do you like being hurt?"

"No," I whispered.

"Then don't make me hurt you." Her tone was no longer a threat—it was a promise.

I looked at them, the weight of their offer like an anchor. No escape. Finally, I nodded. "Okay. I'll do it."

Razor smiled, satisfied, and turned away. Blaze's laughter echoed, sickening.

I stayed frozen. That moment changed everything. It wasn't just survival anymore—it was belonging to something darker, something that wouldn't let go.

Chapter 27
Willow

I opened my eyes, memories flooding back—the ones I'd tried to box away. They sat like a heavy weight on my chest, tight and suffocating. Blake watched me, his expression unreadable.

"That's how it started," I whispered. "How I became one of Razor's girls."

The room held its breath, broken only by the faint ticking of a clock. Each tick stretched the silence longer, pressing down on me. Blake said nothing, but his quiet felt like a weight I couldn't escape. I stole a glance at him: lips pressed thin, eyes shadowed, filled with thoughts he kept to himself.

The quiet became unbearable. I stood abruptly, the couch scraping sharply behind me. "I need a moment," I muttered, voice trembling despite myself.

He watched me go, gaze heavy on my back. The door clicked softly, but I still felt his eyes even through the closed space.

In the hallway, I leaned against the cold wall, breath shallow and uneven. My fists clenched, trying to steady the storm inside.

Get it together, Willow. The words barely a whisper, trembling through the silence.

I straightened, stiff and mechanical, then moved to the nearest chair. Gripping its edge so tightly my knuckles whitened,

I closed my eyes, willing the tremors to stop. *This is so embarrassing.*

Footsteps approached. I opened my eyes just as Blake stopped a few steps away, giving me space I wasn't sure I wanted or needed.

"Are you okay?" His voice was gentle, hesitant. "I know it's hard to talk about this."

Wrapping my arms around myself, I admitted, "It's embarrassing."

He tilted his head. "What is?"

I looked down, voice barely steady. "Telling people that no one cares about you... that you're not worthy of love."

He stepped closer, slow and careful, like I might shatter. Stopping just a foot away, his eyes searched mine. "That's not true."

I shook my head, bitterness rising. A short, bitter laugh escaped. "It is. I've accepted it. But saying it out loud… it's still hard."

The words caught, voice cracking. Tears welled and stung. I turned my head, ashamed, but they came anyway—silent at first, then shaking sobs I couldn't hold back.

"I'm sorry," I choked, breath hitching. "I'm so embarrassing today. You must think I'm a fool."

He stepped closer, steady and quiet, as if he knew I was seconds from falling apart. His eyes softened with something unfamiliar—gentleness, maybe mercy. Reaching out, his hand slipped under my chin with a tenderness I wasn't used to. Warm and grounding, his touch cracked the weight pressing down on me just slightly. I hadn't realized how cold I'd become until that warmth reminded me what it felt like. For a brief moment... I wasn't broken. I was just held.

Chapter 28
Blake

The world froze, thick and blurred, as I stared into Willow's tear-filled eyes. Beyond sadness, I saw years of pain, quiet desperation, a belief she was unworthy of better. It struck deep—how could anyone make her feel like this? How did she not see the strength radiating beneath her doubt?

I swallowed hard. She's stronger than she knows. More beautiful than she realizes.

But inside me, a storm raged. One part said hold back, respect the space between us. Another screamed she needed to hear the truth—that she was worth more than her scars.

The struggle was unbearable. I fought it, but before I could think, my body acted on instinct.

I leaned in, lips brushing hers in a gentle, tentative kiss.

Chapter 29
Willow

My breath caught. For a moment, my mind went blank. All that existed was the warmth of his lips, the soft pressure, the faint scent of his cologne cocooning me. Shock and disbelief melted away as I leaned in, hand instinctively resting on his chest. His arms slid around my waist, hands settling on my lower back, pulling me closer. The kiss deepened.

Outside, the world ceased. No past, no future—just us, caught in an intimacy I hadn't expected but somehow needed more than I dared admit. His lips were gentle, unhurried, every movement deliberate and tender.

When he pulled back, it was slow, reluctant, like he too was fighting something inside. Forehead resting briefly against mine, then stepping away. His breath was uneven, guilt flickering in his deep blue eyes.

"I shouldn't have done that," he said softly. "I know I crossed the line. I'll... ask for your case to be reassigned."

I shook my head, hand reaching out to touch his arm. "No. Please don't. You're the only one I've opened up to. I feel comfortable with you."

His gaze wavered, torn between duty and wanting to do right. "This can't happen again," he said firmly, though hesitation lingered. "It's not allowed."

I nodded, swallowing the weight of his words. "Okay."

He forced a strained smile and stepped back. "Well, the session's over. Good luck at community college."

"Thanks," I replied quietly, voice hollow. The weight of everything suddenly crushed me. Turning, I walked away, unable to look back. My footsteps faded down the hallway as the door clicked shut.

Chapter 30
Blake

I stayed where I was, watching her walk away. I sighed heavily, running a hand through my hair, trying to shake off the tension.

That shouldn't have happened, I chastised myself, willing my thoughts to clear. It can't happen again.

The door closed with a soft click. I didn't move right away.

Cherry lip gloss.

Her taste still lingered on my lips. Sweet. Soft. Unexpectedly intoxicating. Far better than I could have imagined.

I stared at my reflection for a moment longer than I should have. Cold eyes. Perfectly groomed. Measured. But beneath it, there's something else now, something feral clawing at the inside of my ribs.

I closed my eyes and inhaled, slow and deep. Control. Discipline. Distance.

I sat, slowly. The room felt quieter than usual, too quiet. My pen hovered over the page of Willow's file, but I didn't write yet.

Instead, I breathed.

Controlled. Professional. Measured.

I'd built my life on those three pillars. But today... one cracked.

I kissed her.

I told myself it would never happen. I told myself I could control it. Her. Me. But there I was, my hand on her jaw, her breath catching, and I took what I shouldn't have. And worse? She let me. Didn't pull away. Didn't flinch.

That should make it easier to walk away. It didn't.

I exhaled slowly and began to write.

Session #3

Client disclosed significant information regarding her connection to two individuals referred to as "Razor" and "Blaze." Indicates ongoing emotional and physical manipulation by both parties.

Appears to be positioned as a subordinate within

their dynamic, used, controlled, and exposed to unsafe environments.

Eye contact was sustained, if challenging. Body language, jacket wrapped around herself, feet tucked beneath the chair, suggested defensiveness.

The session shifted approximately halfway through when I gently challenged one of her recurring self-deprecating remarks. She stood abruptly and left the office, visibly distressed. She was crying by the time she stepped into the hallway.

I followed.

She didn't go far, stood against a chair in the hallway. Collapsed into it like she was trying to hold herself together with nothing but breath and shame.

In that moment, Willow admitted that no one has ever loved her.

The statement was spoken quietly, as if it had slipped out before she could stop it. But once it was in the air, the silence in the room grew heavy. She wouldn't look at me. Her voice dropped. Her hands trembled.

And seeing her like that, so raw, so open, it *did* something to me.

She wasn't defensive in that moment.

She wasn't hiding behind sarcasm or silence.

She was just… human.

Hurting.

And for the first time since meeting her,

I saw the girl beneath the armor. Not the survivor.

Not the rebel. Just Willow.

When I reached her, I meant only to offer comfort.

A hand on her arm. A steady voice.

But she turned to me, eyes glassy, cheeks streaked, and whispered, "I don't know why it hurts so much to say it."

And I…

I didn't think.

I kissed her.

Just once.

Her lips were warm and trembling, and for a second, she clung to me like I was the only thing keeping her upright. And maybe I was.

I stopped writing, closed the file, as I reminisced in the memory of the kiss.

That kiss… it was crossing a line I had no right to blur.

But when her mouth parted for mine, when she leaned in, when she didn't freeze or flinch or shrink away. I felt something shift in me. Like she gave me permission. Like she could take it.

Like she *wanted* it.

And maybe that's the problem. Because the part of me I'd spent years containing, shaping, suppressing, disguising beneath expensive suits and polished restraint, was beginning to stir.

The beast doesn't wake for just anyone.

She's slipping through the cracks in my walls, slipping past every defence I'd built to keep that part of me locked down.

Though I wondered… if she was *meant* to.

I didn't want to fix her. I wanted to possess her.

To show her that surrender didn't have to mean pain. That control can feel like safety when it's placed in the right hands. *My* hands.

But I can't.

Professional. Controlled. Measured.

These weren't just words. They're the chains I'd bound myself with to protect people like her from men like me.

Still… she didn't run. She didn't pull away. She kissed me back.

Is that a sign she can handle me?

I opened her file again and wrote the closing line.

Therapeutic recommendations:

Client displayed significant emotional vulnerability for the first time. Revealed core wound related to perceived unworthiness of love. Strong emotional reaction followed by flight response. Recommend allowing space for trust repair, slower pacing, and high therapist self-awareness.

Then I closed the file.

And lock the drawer.

And for the first time in years…

I'm not sure that's going to be enough.

Chapter 31
Willow

I let out a long sigh stepping onto the community college campus. The buildings were dull and uninspiring, the air thick with the stale smell of chalk and cafeteria food—a mixture that seemed to settle on everything. Groups of students moved through the courtyards, their voices merging into a constant buzz.

I clenched my fists, forcing myself to calm down. One good thing about hanging out with Razor and Blaze? I got kicked out of every school we ever attended. But here I was again, stuck at another mandated step to "fix my life."

The classroom was as dreary as the rest of the campus, rows of desks lined up before a tired chalkboard. I slid into an empty seat near the back, moving quickly and deliberately, avoiding any eye contact. Just keep to myself and get through today.

I hate school. Slumping further in my chair, I rolled my eyes and crossed my arms tightly over my chest. Let's just get this over with.

The lecturer droned on in a monotone voice. The girl next to me looked half-asleep, struggling with the same boredom. The hours crawled like days.

Finally, when the break was announced, I sprang from my seat. I needed fresh air—away from the stale classroom and the ticking clock.

Wandering aimlessly, I found a small garden tucked behind the main building. It was a quiet sanctuary with a few benches shaded by tall trees. The distant hum of traffic was softened by birdsong and buzzing insects.

I sat on a bench and unwrapped my meager lunch—a half sandwich with butter—but my mind wasn't on food.

Blake. The memory of his kiss washed over me—a confusing mix of warmth and uncertainty. I bit my lip, suppressing the small smile tugging at my mouth.

He probably regrets it. The thought came instantly, swirling with doubt.

Why would he kiss me? I'm not the kind of girl you bring home. Not worth that kind of attention. Not from someone like him.

Shaking my head, I forced myself to focus on the sandwich. There was another session ahead. No time to spiral—not today.

Chapter 32
Willow

Class felt just as dull the second time around. Settling into my seat, I noticed my usual neighbor replaced by a familiar face.

A guy strutted in with a cocky swagger—dark hair tied into a messy man bun, strands falling over his face. His leather jacket added an edge, paired with ripped black jeans and a tight white shirt that hugged his frame.

"Fancy meeting you here," he said, a teasing grin spreading as he slid in beside me.

I frowned. "What are you doing sitting here?"

"Your neighbor didn't take much persuading," he smirked. "A pack of smokes and the seat was mine."

I rolled my eyes. "Seriously?"

Braxton chuckled, unfazed. "Best pack I ever spent."

Leaning back, arms crossed, I studied him skeptically. "What's your angle?"

"No angle," he shrugged, smile widening. "Just thought you looked like a cool chick. Wanted to get to know you."

His tone was light, almost genuine, but it didn't fool me.

"Was glad to see you in class today," he added casually. "I was dreading it, but now I think I might actually enjoy finishing school."

I ignored him, focusing on the teacher. My annoyance didn't seem to register with him. Maybe if I ignored him long enough, he'd get the hint.

"You not going to talk to me today, Floss?" he asked, leaning closer, cocky grin in place.

I slammed my book shut, crossing my arms. "You got me confused with someone else. My name's not Floss."

He laughed. "I know. It's my nickname for you." He nodded toward my hair.

I raised a skeptical eyebrow.

"Your hair's like fairy floss—cotton candy," he explained, never losing the smile.

Great. I rolled my eyes. How old is he?

"Okay," I snapped, irritation creeping in. "What do you want?"

Feigning innocence, he shrugged. "What do you mean?"

"If annoyance and ignoring you don't work, I'll be blunt: I don't have drugs or money. And forget sex—that's not happening."

His easy smile faltered for a moment before returning. "You've got me wrong. I just think you seem cool and wanted to get to know you."

"Right," I huffed. "I'm sure with all your charm, you have plenty of friends. You don't need me."

"Maybe," he said with a grin, leaning back again. "But I want to get to know you."

I muttered, opening my book. "Now shut up and let me listen. I have to pass this class."

Braxton smirked but didn't push further, though I caught his gaze flickering my way with amusement. I fought the urge to roll my eyes again.

What is with this guy?

Chapter 33
Willow

The rest of class passed without incident. Braxton remained a mild distraction but eventually left me alone. I caught him glancing a few times, but I refused to acknowledge him.

When the session ended, I packed quickly, eager to leave the strange encounter behind. Still, a faint curiosity about the confident boy with the cocky grin tugged at me despite my efforts to push it away.

For now, though, I shoved it aside. More pressing matters awaited.

Just survive today. One step at a time.

I slung my bag over my shoulder and stepped into the quad, bathed in the warm glow of late afternoon sun. Students lingered in small groups, laughter and chatter filling the air.

As I navigated the paths, my gaze swept the crowd. Then it landed on a familiar figure leaning against a low brick wall—Braxton, in his usual confident stance, dark leather jacket catching the light.

He chatted with a girl who looked like she belonged in a glossy magazine—perfectly styled hair, a sly, rehearsed smile.

I slowed, slipping closer to the hedges. Peering through the leaves, I caught snippets of their conversation.

"So, you got the stuff?" Braxton's voice was low, casual but edged.

The girl flipped her hair, smiling teasingly. "Did you doubt me?"

Braxton chuckled, a flicker of hesitation in his voice. "So, you got everything I needed?"

She nodded. "He said he's happy to make this a regular thing."

My stomach knotted. Leaning in closer, I caught more.

"I'm not sure I want to change my regular supplier," he admitted. "He didn't have what I wanted this time, but he's normally good."

The girl's smile didn't falter. "Dunk wants to get you as a regular. I can take you to meet him tomorrow night."

A bitter sting hit my chest. I straightened, jaw clenched.

I knew it. He's into that stuff.

I sucked in a breath, pushing down the disappointment. Getting to know him would have been a mistake. I'd made the right call.

Turning to leave, I felt his gaze shift suddenly toward me. A flicker of recognition, maybe guilt.

He nodded, then winked, as if daring me to know I'd been watching.

I huffed, frustration rising as he started walking toward me, still talking to the girl.

I didn't wait. I quickened my pace, determined to put distance between myself and the trouble Braxton carried.

I want a fresh start. No room for that in my life.

Chapter 34
Braxton

Seeing Willow, I cut my conversation short. "Yeah, sounds good. Gotta go," I muttered, turning toward her.

"Hey, Floss!" I called across the quad, jogging slowly to catch up.

She flinched but kept walking.

"Floss, wait up!" I quickened my pace.

She finally stopped, arms crossed tightly. "What do you want, Braxton?"

She used my name. That had to be progress.

Grinning, I ignored her tone. "Feel like some company on your walk home?"

"No thanks," she replied flatly, shifting away.

"Please," I begged, trying an endearing pout.

Her glare hardened. "I told you—I want a fresh start. I don't want trouble." She pointed back. "That over there? That was trouble."

I raised my hands defensively. "It's not what it looks like."

She snorted. "Nope. It never is."

Ignoring my attempts, she started walking again, pace quickening.

I stood frozen, watching her retreat. Her words stung.

She wasn't supposed to see that side. She's got it all wrong. That's not who I am. She won't want anything to do with me now.

She never looked back.

The sun dipped lower, casting a long shadow as she disappeared.

I stood there, wondering if I'd already blown my chance.

Chapter 35
Willow

The kitchen was as chaotic as ever. Brandy's voice echoed through the room, high-pitched and frantic. Across from her, Barb stood with her arms crossed, her expression a mix of defiance and indifference, a cigarette dangling loosely from her fingers.

In between them sat Noah, staring blankly into space, his face unreadable. The worn sleeves of his jumper bunched at his elbows, and his sneakers barely touched the floor.

I lingered in the doorway for a moment, my stomach sinking at the familiar scene. Not again. This apartment had become a broken record—same arguments, same shouting, over and over. Nothing ever changed.

I exhaled slowly, squaring my shoulders as I stepped into the room. My voice, when I spoke, was forced to sound calm and steady.

"Saw Jack outside, why don't you go play ball with him, Noah?"

Noah's vacant stare snapped at the sound of my voice. His eyes widened with uncertainty. He hesitated for a moment, then nodded quickly, grabbing his cap before darting toward the door. His escape was swift, as though the tension in the room was too much to bear.

Once Noah was out of earshot, I turned back to face the battleground, my gaze moving between Brandy and Barb. I crossed my arms, bracing myself for the inevitable. "Okay, what are you two fighting about now?"

Brandy's frustration reached its peak, and she threw her hands in the air. "Barb ate all the bread, AGAIN!!"

"And?" Barb shot back, her voice cool and dismissive, as if this was part of some never-ending routine. "It's my house, isn't it?"

Brandy's jaw tightened, her hands clenching into fists as she glared at Barb. "Now I can't make Noah a sandwich!" she spat.

Barb didn't flinch. She simply leaned against the counter, arms still crossed, looking completely indifferent to the argument—or anyone in the room.

But Brandy wasn't done. She jabbed a finger at Barb, her tone sharp. "That money you get from the department is supposed to be for food and clothes! Not to fund your gambling habit and buy your smokes!"

The noise in the room buzzed in my ears, the sheer volume of their bickering making my head throb. Brandy still didn't realize it would never change—Barb was a hollow shell of a person, always putting her own needs first.

Before Barb could fire back, I stepped in, trying to defuse the situation. "Don't worry, I've got a few bucks. I'll go get some bread."

Barb's eyes flicked toward me, a smirk curling at the edges of her lips. "About time you made yourself useful," she mocked sarcastically. "I'm surprised they didn't just lock you up with the rest of them."

Her words hit like a slap.

"Come on, Brandy, let's get out of here."

Brandy didn't hesitate. She stormed out behind me, the door slamming shut with a loud thud as we stepped into the quiet corridor.

As we walked, the unease that had been gnawing at me all week refused to let go. Razor's warning echoed in my mind like a broken record. She might be behind bars for now, but I knew better than to think that made me safe. The streets felt different now—less familiar, more menacing.

I had to stay strong. I had to believe her threat was just a bluff, a desperate attempt to scare me.

But what if it wasn't?

The trial was only days away. I just had to hold on until then. If things went the way they were supposed to, Razor would be locked up for a long time.

But if they didn't?

If Razor got out, I'd have no choice but to run. Hide somewhere she couldn't find me. But where?

I shoved the thought aside as we reached the corner store, trying to focus on something simple. Bread. Just get the bread.

I scanned the shelves as we walked down the aisles, mentally calculating what I could afford. Brandy trailed behind me, arms crossed, her eyes already darting toward the candy and make up aisles, her gaze lingering on the shelves with the hope of a treat.

"I should have enough to grab two loaves."

Brandy perked up, her step light and bouncy when she saw the row of lip glosses.

"How about a lip gloss?" I glanced back at her with a mischievous smile.

Her enthusiasm was contagious, and for a second, I felt my own mood lift. "I'll grab some nail polish too. Haven't painted my nails in ages."

Brandy clapped her hands in delight. "You totally should! You deserve a little treat now and then."

I shrugged, trying to ignore the warmth spreading in my chest at her excitement. "Come on, let's go."

We made it to the checkout line. It wasn't long, but that gnawing unease settled back over me as we waited. The cashier, a girl with a bored expression and a ponytail, scanned our items one by one.

Chewing gum she looked at us with an emotionless stare. "That's $6.50," she held out her hand.

I fumbled in my pocket, pulling out the crumpled bills I had left. My stomach dropped. "Oh, sorry," I tugged at the sleeve of my shirt. "I only have five bucks. Just leave the nail polish, please."

Before the cashier could say anything, a voice interrupted, "I'll get that for you."

I recognized that voice.

Braxton.

I froze, my jaw clenching for a moment before I rolled my eyes and turned to face him, a stern look on my face. His cocky grin was already in place, his hoodie slung low over one brow like he owned the place.

Brandy, on the other hand, practically melted. Her grin spread wide, the familiar gleam of interest in her eyes as she leaned in just a little closer to him, twirling a lock of her hair.

"No," I crossed my arms in protest. "I'll just leave the nail polish, thank you."

Braxton shrugged, unfazed. "Come on, it's only a buck fifty."

"I don't want to owe you anything," I shot back, irritation sharpening my tone.

Brandy tugged at my sleeve, her voice soft and pleading. "Come on, Wills, you haven't gotten anything for yourself in ages."

"Shut up, Brandy," I snapped before I could stop myself. The words came out harsher than I intended, but I was too frustrated to care.

Brandy flinched, muttering something under her breath as she looked away. I turned back to the cashier. "Just the bread and the lip gloss, thanks."

Braxton wasn't giving up. He stepped closer, his tone now softer, almost coaxing. "Let me buy it for you. Call it a peace offering for annoying you so much."

I glared at him, crossing my arms tighter. "I said, no, thank you."

His smile faltered, and for a brief moment, I almost felt bad. But there was no way I was letting him wear me down.

Not this time.

"Come on, Brandy," I grabbed the bread and headed for the door.

Brandy hesitated, her gaze flicking back toward Braxton as I pulled at her arm to leave the store. I had enough on my plate already.

The alleyway was drenched in darkness, littered with the usual debris from the nearby dumpsters. The air stank of rotting food, mingling with the sharp, bitter scent of cigarette smoke. A flickering streetlight hung overhead, casting a weak, yellowish glow over the narrow path. The distant hum of the city buzzed somewhere far beyond, but in this alley, it felt like another world entirely—isolated, suffocating.

Brandy and I lingered near the dumpster, trying to blend into the shadows, hoping to avoid the chaos of the streets and make our way home unnoticed. But I couldn't shake the rising tension that crawled beneath my skin, gnawing at me from the inside out.

Brandy, oblivious to the storm brewing in my chest, prattled on about the good-looking guy she'd seen at the shops. Why wouldn't I let him buy me the nail polish? Her voice grated on me, distracting me, pulling me further from the edge of control. Even when Braxton wasn't around, he still managed to find ways to get under my skin.

"Enough already, Brandy," I exhaled sharply, trying to shake off the unease building inside me.

She looked at me, her lips curling into a playful pout, her hoop earrings glinting faintly in the dim light. "But he was so nice!" she protested, her eyes lighting up with the memory. "And he was *so* hot."

I rubbed my forehead, frustrated. "Enough, Brandy."

She grinned, flipping her hair over her shoulder. "If you're not interested, I'll have him."

I rolled my eyes. "He's trouble. Stay away from him."

But before she could respond, a figure emerged from the shadows—one I'd hoped never to see again. The thug from community service. His presence hit me like a cold wave, and the smirk twisting his lips only made it worse. The tattoo peeking from under his collar made my skin crawl.

"Fancy bumping into you here," his voice was smooth and predatory, sending a chill down my spine.

I froze, the blood draining from my face. A shiver crept up my back as he stepped closer.

"Brandy, run home now," I hissed, the urgency in my voice cracking. The words tumbled out before I could think.

Brandy shot me a confused look. "What?"

"NOW!" I shouted, my voice sharp with panic, leaving no room for debate.

She didn't hesitate. Without another word, she turned and bolted down the alley, her footsteps echoing in the still night. But I couldn't bring myself to watch her go. My eyes remained fixed on the guy in front of me.

"Real charmer, huh?" I forced the words out, trying to hide the tremor in my voice, but failing.

He didn't answer. Instead, he took another step closer, his eyes gleaming with amusement. "She's cute," he remarked casually, never once glancing in the direction Brandy had disappeared. His gaze remained locked on mine, too intense to ignore.

I squared my shoulders, trying to hold my ground. "Leave her alone."

"She's done nothing wrong. You can do whatever you want to me, but leave her out of it."

His laugh was dark, cruel. "Nobody tells Razor what to do," he sneered, his grin twisting into something more sinister. "You should know that by now."

I felt paralyzed as he stepped closer, his presence suffocating. The world seemed to shrink until it was just him and me. He stopped just inches away, and I could feel the heat of his breath against my skin. My heart hammered in my chest.

"Hmmm... you smell good," he murmured, his voice low and rasping, sending a wave of revulsion through me.

His finger traced slowly up my arm, then along my neck, before his hand cupped my face. Every inch of my skin burned under his touch.

"Hope Razor lets me have some fun with you," he whispered, his words hanging heavy in the air. "Before she does away with you."

Terror surged through me, but my mouth went dry, and I couldn't find the voice to scream. His touch felt suffocating, like it was slowly draining the life out of me.

Finally, he stepped back, releasing me from his grip. A twisted smile curled his lips. "Until we meet again, sweet cheeks."

I was stunned. His footsteps echoed in the emptiness, growing fainter, until all that was left was silence. The alley felt colder now, like a void had opened, swallowing everything around me. The darkness seemed to close in.

Tears welled up in my eyes, and before I could stop them, they began to fall. "What have I done?" I whispered to myself, my voice trembling. "I should've just gone to jail." The thought of being locked away—away from all this—seemed almost comforting. "What does it matter anyway? Nobody wants me."

I collapsed against the dumpster, sobbing uncontrollably, my body shaking with grief and helplessness. Maybe it would be easier if Razor just finished me off.

But then, a voice broke through the darkness, pulling me from my spiraling thoughts. "Floss, is that you?"

I looked up, startled. There, standing at the entrance of the alley, was Braxton. His presence felt like a beacon in the darkness, though I wasn't sure I wanted it.

He rushed toward me, his face etched with concern. "Are you okay?"

I flinched as his arms reached for me, pulling me into a hug. I didn't want his comfort. I didn't want to feel anything right now. But for some reason, I didn't pull away. My arms hung limp at my sides. I couldn't bring myself to respond, my emotions too tangled to unravel.

What am I doing?

After a moment, I pushed him away, my body stiff with resistance. "Don't touch me," I snapped, sharper than I intended. "You can't just come up and touch people like that."

Braxton looked taken aback, his face falling into confusion. "I'm sorry, Floss. You just looked upset."

I glared at him, frustration bubbling over. "And stop calling me Floss," I huffed, exasperated.

Without waiting for his response, I turned and stormed away, my feet pounding against the concrete. Every part of me screamed to run, to get away from him, from everything. To just disappear.

Chapter 36
Braxton

I heard her before I saw her—those quiet, gut-wrenching sobs drifting from the alley, hitting me like a punch to the ribs. When I stepped around the corner and saw her there, crumpled against the dumpster, my heart sank.

It wasn't just the tears. It was the look in her eyes that hit hardest. Wide. Glassy. Haunted.

Not just scared. Shattered.

That kind of fear doesn't come from shadows or cheap horror flicks. No, that's the kind of fear life beats into you. I've seen it before. Too many damn times. It never gets easier.

I went to her slowly, carefully, like approaching a scared animal, and when I pulled her into my arms, she didn't fight me—not at first. She just folded. Limp. Small. Like she didn't have the strength to hold herself together anymore.

Damn! It shattered something inside me.

Holding her like that, feeling her tremble against me... I wanted to promise her the world. Tell her she was safe now. That I'd fix it. Whatever "it" was. That she didn't have to carry this burden alone anymore.

But just as quickly as she let me in, she remembered. Remembered who she was. What the world had taught her. And in a heartbeat, she pulled away.

Pushed me back, like my arms burned her. Like closeness was a danger she couldn't afford. Her guard slammed back into place so fast it felt like whiplash.

She couldn't let herself lean on anyone. Not even for a second. And I get it. I do.

But damn, it doesn't make it hurt any less. Doesn't make me want to walk away. If anything, it makes me want to stay...

Long enough to show her that not everyone leaves. Not me. Not this time.

With one last, reluctant breath, I told myself I couldn't win her over. But something deep inside whispered that I had to try. Something inside me knew she was worth fighting for.

I rubbed the back of my neck, still standing in the spot where she'd left me. My eyes strained to catch one final glimpse of her. But she was gone.

I wondered, almost out of habit, if I'd ever see her again.

She's carved her name into my silence.

Chapter 37
Willow

I lay in bed, my body heavy, drained by everything that had happened today. Blake's kiss kept replaying in my mind, how gentle and unexpected it had been. And then there was everything with Braxton. The gut-wrenching realization that he wasn't any different from what I'd feared. He was trouble—I could see it clear as day— but the way he rushed to comfort me in the alley had thrown me off. It wasn't like any reaction I was used to from the guys around here. And maybe that's exactly why I should stay away.

And then the man in the alley. The way he leaned in so close, his breath on me. The chilling words that made my stomach twist in knots. I should've run. I should've done more to protect myself and Brandy, but instead, I froze.

Now, in the quiet of my room, all I could do was think. Was there even a way out of this mess I'd gotten myself into? Could I escape everything? From him? From them? The weight of it all pressed down on me like a suffocating blanket.

I turned over, staring at the ceiling, trying to clear my mind, but the thoughts wouldn't stop. I couldn't leave Noah. Not now. He was the only thing I still had to hold onto. The thought of abandoning him was unbearable. But the truth was, I was running out of options.

Suddenly, the vibration of my phone on the nightstand broke the silence. I picked it up, glancing at the screen. Blake.

I sat up, my heart picking up speed. Blake. After everything that had happened, I hadn't expected to hear from him again. My fingers hovered over the screen as I opened the message, my breath catching in my throat.

"I know I shouldn't be messaging you. I just can't stop thinking about you since the kiss."

I stared at the words, my chest tightening. Was this real? Or was I dreaming? I didn't even know anymore.

I quickly typed back. "Yes, you've also been on my mind."

A small smile tugged at my lips as I sent it, my fingers trembling slightly. I didn't know what was happening, but for the first time in a long while, I felt something other than fear and confusion. I felt… hope?

His response came almost immediately.

"How was college?"

I sighed, leaning back against the pillows. College. Wasn't that supposed to be some kind of escape? A chance for something more?

"It was okay. It's school, you know. It sucks."

I could almost hear his chuckle on the other end.

"Yeah, I wouldn't want to go back. It will, however, set you up for a job and get you out of that place, though."

His words were kind, reassuring in their simplicity. But they didn't change the reality I was living in. Still, I appreciated the sentiment.

"I know. Thanks."

There was a brief pause before his next message appeared.

"Thanks for what?"

I hesitated. Should I say it? I didn't want to seem too vulnerable, too open. But the truth was, I was grateful for him. For the way he'd been there for me today, for making me feel like I wasn't completely alone.

"For being there for me today. You don't have to. It's not your job."

His reply came swiftly, and I could almost feel his smile through the text.

"With you. You make it too easy. I don't even have to think about it. Looking forward to seeing you again tomorrow."

I didn't know how to respond. I wanted to say something, but my heart was a jumble of emotions, none of which I could make sense of.

Before I could think of anything else to say, another message from him popped up.

"Sorry, that was too much. Night."

I sat there for a moment, staring at the screen. Part of me wanted to respond, to tell him it wasn't too much. But another part of me, the one that had been burned before, warned me to tread carefully.

"Night Blake."

I set my phone down on the nightstand, the glow from the screen fading as I sank back into the bed. I stared at the ceiling again, my thoughts swirling. Blake was sweet. He made me feel good. But he also made me vulnerable, and that terrified me.

We can't let it happen again. The kiss. The feelings. If the judge or the detective found out about it, they could revoke my conditions. I couldn't afford that. I had to keep my head on straight, even if my heart wanted to do otherwise.

I closed my eyes, trying to push the thoughts from my mind. But the images of Blake, his smile, the way he looked at me, lingered.

I rolled over, pulling the covers closer to me. I needed sleep, needed to escape this whirlwind of emotions. But as I drifted off, I couldn't shake the nagging feeling that things were only going to get more complicated from here.

I walked into Blake's office, my nerves on edge. I had no idea what to expect after yesterday's kiss and the texts that followed. My palms were sweaty, a lump forming in my throat. The unease of not knowing what today's session would hold settled heavily in my chest. I quickly glanced over at Blake as I entered. He was already seated, looking almost as uncomfortable as I felt. His usual calm, confident posture was gone, replaced by a slight tension, as if he was just as unsure of how to break the silence as I was.

"Morning, Willow," his voice was softer than usual.

I smiled faintly, trying to ease the tension between us. "Morning," I whispered, my voice barely audible.

Blake relaxed a little, his eyes meeting mine with a softness that was almost reassuring. "It's good to see you," he added, shifting in his seat again, his gaze still searching mine, waiting for some sign of how to proceed.

I nodded quickly, feeling a swirl of emotions inside me. I didn't know what to expect seeing him today, but there was something about his presence that felt... comforting. Still, everything that had happened between us over the past few days had thrown me off balance, and I wasn't sure where things stood.

Blake tilted his head slightly, offering a tentative smile. "Do you want to get straight into it?" His eyes scanned my face, searching for any sign of discomfort.

I hesitated for a moment, then took a deep breath and nodded, trying to steady myself.

"Yeah," I choked out, clearing my thoughts. "Let's do it."

The air between us felt thick, heavy. Blake glanced at me again, waiting, unsure how to break the silence.

I crossed my legs and leaned back on the couch, trying to settle into the moment. "So," I began, my voice soft, "what do you want to talk about today?"

Blake shifted in his chair, tapping his fingers nervously on his knee. "We could pick up where we left off yesterday... if you feel comfortable with that," he suggested, his voice cautious, careful not to push me too hard.

I swallowed hard, the memory of the kiss still fresh in my mind. "Not sure that's a good idea," the words came out more spontaneously. "Especially if that's not suppose to happen again." A small smirk tugged at the edges of my lips.

Blake's face flushed slightly, clearly embarrassed. "I didn't mean the kiss," his expression quickly shifted from shock to apologetic. "I meant... talking about Razor and Blaze," he clarified.

I couldn't help but giggle, the tension in my shoulders easing as laughter bubbled up. "I know," I shook my head gently. A small, genuine smile spread across my lips. "I was just joking."

Blake let out a relieved breath, a smile tugging at his own lips. "Oh," his expression softened as he looked at me. "Okay, well, if you're comfortable with it, I'll ask the questions."

I nodded, feeling the tension lift a little. Leaning forward, I set my hands on my knees and looked at him with a steady gaze. "Sure, ask away."

Blake shifted in his seat, his eyes never leaving me as he spoke. "How did your friendship with Razor and Blaze develop from there?"

I leaned further back into the couch, gripping my knees lightly as I took a moment to collect my thoughts. The familiar weight of my past settled over me, but I pushed through it. "We ended up in detention together a lot," I murmured, not managing to get my voice much above a whisper.

"Somehow, that doesn't surprise me," Blake remarked, a small smile tugging at the corners of his mouth. I couldn't help but mirror his expression, nervously tucking a loose strand of hair behind my ear.

"Yeah," I said, my voice quiet as the memories rushed back. "It started small. They'd ask me to cover for them when they left early, or take the blame for things they got caught doing. It kind of escalated from there."

Blake's face grew more serious as he listened, his eyes narrowing slightly. "What else did you do for them?"

I shifted uncomfortably, feeling the weight of my past actions pressing in on me. "I covered for a lot of things," I mumbled, the words slipping out before I could stop them. "I helped them with... jobs. Being the lure. Getting targets to let their guard down... making sure they were never hungry."

Blake's brow furrowed, his eyes scanning mine with a quiet intensity. "And in return?"

I exhaled, the heaviness of it all settling deeper. "In return," I said with a heavy sigh, "they protected me. In my neighborhood, protection was everything." I stared at the floor, the shame pulling at me. "The guys there... they don't take no for an answer. But with Razor and Blaze, I was off-limits. No one messed with them, or their girls. So, I could walk the streets without worrying... mostly."

Blake nodded slowly, digesting my words. "Did you have a problem with this before Razor came into the picture?"

I kept my gaze lowered, feeling the sting of shame. "You could say that."

I felt Blake lean forward slightly, his voice soft but probing. "Someone hurt you?"

My heart stuttered in my chest. I snapped my gaze up at him, sharp breath catching in my throat. "I wasn't raped, if that's what you're getting at," I snapped. "I always knew what they wanted. I always knew." My arms crossed defensively around my chest. "But I'm no angel. There are things I needed... and I had no money. I'm not proud of it, but in my world, it's a form of currency. That is, unless the guys don't just take what they want when they want it. But... that's just how it is. We all know it. We just have to accept it."

Blake recoiled slightly, his face softening with an expression I couldn't quite read, but he didn't interrupt. I pushed forward, my voice growing steadier as I let the truth spill out—truths I'd buried for far too long.

"You use whatever advantages you have." The bitterness in my words matched the hardening of my gaze. "So yeah, I had sex with guys. Not because I wanted to, but because I had to. It wasn't enjoyable... but it was necessary. And it got me what I needed to survive."

A heavy silence fell between us. Blake's eyes were sad, yet filled with understanding. He seemed to wrestle with what I'd just confessed. Finally, he spoke, his tone quieter, gentler. "This might be a little personal," he said, his features shifting to something uncertain. "You don't have to answer if you don't feel comfortable."

I nodded, my emotions swirling inside me. I felt his concern like a weight, and despite myself, I trusted him. "Okay," I said, bracing for whatever was to come next.

Blake's voice softened even more. "Have you ever slept with someone... because you wanted to? Not because you needed to?"

His words hung in the air, heavy and piercing. I found myself at a loss for how to respond. I'd never allowed myself to think about it that way—not once.

Sex had never been about that for me. Not ever. My mind was a tangled mess of emotions, and the thought of answering... I couldn't do it. I just shook my head.

Blake immediately backpedaled, remorse flashing across his face. "Sorry."

"You don't have to answer that," he said quickly, his voice laced with regret. "I just wanted to understand... your life, what you've been through, what you've experienced." His hand lifted in an apologetic gesture, pulling away.

I turned my gaze away, embarrassment flooding me. I'd never been this open with anyone before.

Blake stood up, his shoulders slumped, a hint of self-doubt in his posture. He walked over to me, his voice softer. "Sorry, Willow," he murmured. "I got too personal. You weren't ready."

I looked up at him, my heart heavy, but I managed a small smile. I didn't want him to feel bad. "It's okay. I understand why you'd ask," I said quietly. The words didn't sit right on my tongue, but I needed him to understand.

The shame began to creep back in, twisting inside me. "I just... it's not something I'm proud of," I mumbled, feeling the discomfort in my own words.

Blake sat back down, his gaze steady and unwavering. "I told you, I won't judge you," he said, his voice firm yet gentle. "I'm here to understand you. To understand how you got to where you are today."

I took a deep breath, gathering myself. I knew this was the moment where I had to face the truth, no matter how painful it was. "I've only ever had sex to get something I needed... or to get out of trouble," I admitted, feeling the weight of the words. "I've never found someone I wanted to just be with."

Blake's face softened with a sadness that resonated deep within me.

"Don't do that!" I snapped, my voice breaking through the thick silence. "Don't look at me like I'm broken."

"Is that what I'm doing?" Blake asked quietly.

I sighed deeply, rubbing my face with both hands.

"I can't believe you've never had a guy sweep you off your feet," Blake muttered, rubbing the back of his neck. His eyes widened in disbelief. "Never?"

I let out a dry laugh, bitterness seeping into my words. "Yeah, because I'm such a catch."

Blake stood up and walked toward me, his eyes never leaving mine. He reached out, his hand steady as he gently pulled me up from the couch. Our faces were inches apart, and I could feel the heat of his gaze, intense and unyielding.

"You tell me not to see you as broken," he said, frustration lining his words, "but that's all you do. You put yourself down all the time. You're incredibly strong, Willow. For everything you've been through, you're still standing. I can't stand that you don't see how beautiful and strong you are. If I can't see you as broken, then you can't either."

His words hit me like a tidal wave. My chest tightened, my heart pounded, and emotion surged through me so fast it left me dizzy. And before I could stop myself, before the fear could stop me, I kissed him.

It wasn't careful. It wasn't planned. It was desperate, raw—every part of me had been waiting for that one moment of madness. His mouth met mine with equal urgency, a collision of heat and hunger, of two people too tired of being alone.

Something inside me cracked open.

For the first time in so long, I didn't feel like a burden. I didn't feel invisible. With his lips on mine, I felt wanted. Like I mattered.

But then he pulled back.

The loss of him was instant. Like stepping from warmth into cold.

"We can't," his voice was strained, rough with emotion. His hands cradled my face, thumbs brushing my skin as though he couldn't bear to let go. "Even if we could... I'm not good for you."

I stood there, speechless. The weight of everything pressed down on me, heavy and confusing. I didn't know what to say. All I knew was that kiss had made me feel alive. And now, I was left reeling, wondering if I'd just imagined it meant something more.

Chapter 38
Blake

She looked at me like I was something worth holding onto. That terrified me more than anything.

I wanted to kiss her again. To pull her in and drown in the feeling she gave me. Her lips had awakened something inside me—something raw, something feral.

Her kiss tasted like hope. Like fire and rain. And it wrecked me.

Because I saw her.

I saw every broken piece she tried so hard to hide, every shadow behind those stunning blue eyes. And for a moment, I let myself believe I could be the one to protect her.

But I know what I am.

I can't be her safe place. I'm not made for soft things. I don't fix people. I burn them.

Still, when she kissed me, it felt like the beginning of something I couldn't stop. I wanted to be better. For her.

Not just because she deserved more, but because she made me want to be more.

But desire isn't enough.

So, I stepped back. I lied to both of us when I said I wasn't good for her. The truth? She's the only good thing that's touched me in years.

Chapter 39
Willow

He stepped back, looking torn, as though he couldn't decide if he was fighting himself or something else.

"Blake," I whispered, barely finding my voice, gripping his shirt.

He hesitated for only a second, then his hands were back on my face, his lips crashing into mine with a force that stole the air from my lungs.

It was different this time. Wilder. Hotter. Like every ounce of restraint he'd held onto shattered, and he was done pretending.

My back hit the wall as he pressed into me, his body solid, commanding, overwhelming in the best way. I clung to him, my fingers knotting in his shirt, desperate to hold onto the feeling.

He made me feel wanted. Craved. Cherished. Like I was more than just a name on a file. More than some girl with a past.

Every touch burned into me. His hands moved with purpose—not asking permission, but giving me everything I didn't know I needed. My mind emptied, leaving only sensation—the scrape of his stubble, the warmth of his breath, the pressure of his body.

And in that moment, I wasn't broken. I was his.

Chapter 40
Blake

I lost control.

I'm not sure when it happened—maybe when she whispered my name, maybe when her fingers tangled in my shirt like she never wanted to let go.

All I knew was that the beast inside me—the one I'd buried under rules and routines and years of silence—was awake.

And she was feeding it.

When I lifted her, her legs wrapped around me instinctively, like she belonged there. The way she looked at me, wide-eyed, lips swollen from our kiss, cheeks flushed, I almost lost myself.

She has no idea what she's doing to me.

No idea that every sound she makes, every shiver, every breathless gasp drives me deeper into the fire.

My lips found her neck, her shoulder, the curve of her throat. I needed to taste her. To mark her. To own this moment.

Because for the first time in my life, I didn't feel out of control.

I felt alive.

Then the knock came.

Sharp. Brutal. Reality tore through the heat.

We froze. Still tangled up in each other, still panting like we were halfway through a storm.

Just like that, the moment shattered.

She looked at me like she was confused—was this all a mistake? And I looked back at her, wondering how the hell I was ever going to let her go.

Chapter 41
Willow

We stood there in stunned silence, the room heavy with unspoken words. My chest rose and fell with each breath, my heart pounding against my ribs. My cheeks burned, and I instinctively raised a trembling hand to my face, trying to regain some composure. I wasn't sure what to say, or how to bridge the sudden gap that had opened between us.

Blake was the first to speak, his voice soft but edged with awkwardness, as if he was scrambling to regain control. He rubbed the back of his neck, glancing toward the door.

"That must be my next client," he said, his expression flashing apologetically—though I couldn't tell if it was for the interruption or what had just happened between us.

I cleared my throat, forcing myself to focus. My thoughts were still a jumbled mess, but I needed to regain some semblance of control.

"I have community service. I can't be late," The words tumbled out before I had time to think. My voice trembled, betraying the nerves I was trying to suppress.

Blake gave me a small, teasing smile, stepping closer just enough that I could feel his presence again. His eyes locked onto mine.

"Until next time," he smirked. But there was something beneath those words—something deeper—that made my stomach flutter.

I returned his smile, though mine felt shaky, a mix of emotions swirling inside me. Part of me wanted to stay, to linger in the warmth of what we'd just shared. But another part knew I couldn't. I had responsibilities to face—things I couldn't ignore, no matter how much I wanted to lose myself in him.

"Yeah," I muttered, as if I was trying to convince myself more than him.

His expression softened. For a fleeting moment, I thought I saw something vulnerable in his gaze. Then, with a playful wink, he added, "Until then," his words carrying a hint of finality that left me yearning for more. I turned to leave, my hand reaching for the door. Just as I pushed it open, I glanced back over my shoulder. He was still watching me, his gaze intense, as though memorizing every detail of me in that moment.

For a fleeting second, I wondered, *What might've happened if we hadn't been interrupted? If we'd let the fire between us burn just a little longer?*

But I shook the thought away. I had things to do—obligations that wouldn't wait. Yet, even as I stepped out of the room, a part of me couldn't help but anticipate tomorrow, wondering what would happen the next time I saw him.

Leaving Blake's office, my mind was a chaotic whirlwind of emotions. The kiss lingered on my lips, a memory too vivid to shake.

The connection—the unspoken tension between us—was overwhelming, almost suffocating. I tried to steady my breathing as the bus rattled along its route, the world outside a blur.

When the vehicle finally came to a halt, I stepped off and forced myself to focus on the dull grey building in front of me: the community service center. The sight snapped me back to reality. I didn't have the luxury of dwelling on Blake or the firestorm he'd stirred inside me. Time was ticking, and I barely made it before being late.

Heads above everyone else was Frank, the ever-sarcastic community service coordinator, his arms crossed as he surveyed the group. His expression was one of amused disapproval—a mix that seemed to be his default setting. "Hello, unlawful ladies and lads," he began, his voice dripping with dry humor. I couldn't help but roll my eyes. His dramatic greetings were as predictable as they were unnecessary.

"Today," Frank continued, pacing in front of us like a drill sergeant, "we'll be helping out at the local soup kitchen. Hope you like potatoes and onions, because you'll be peeling and chopping a lot of them."

The groan that escaped me was barely audible.

"Great," I muttered, more resigned than bitter. It wasn't that I minded the work itself. I just wasn't in the mood—not after the emotional chaos I'd just left behind.

If Frank noticed—or cared—about my muttered sarcasm, he gave no indication. Instead, he clapped his hands together and delivered the next bombshell with Frank's typical enthusiasm.

"I also hope you got friendly with your partner from the other day. It went so well that I've decided, during your community service, this will be your permanent partner."

The words hit me like a bucket of ice water. Permanent partner! My stomach dropped. I had no interest in being tethered to anyone here, least of all Braxton.

My gaze slid reluctantly toward him. Of course, he was already looking at me, that infuriatingly bright cocky grin plastered across his smug face like he'd just won the lottery.

"Perfect," I muttered sarcastically.

Braxton, oblivious to my displeasure—or perhaps deliberately ignoring it—practically bounced on his feet.

"Yes!" He fist pumped. His enthusiasm made me cringe. "Happy to be working with you, partner!"

I rolled my eyes again, biting back a sigh. This was going to be a long day.

Frank, meanwhile, was unmoved by the dynamics playing out in front of him.

"Get on the bus," he ordered sharply, "we head off in five." With that, he turned and headed to the bus, his lecture now complete.

As I trudged toward the bus, the weight of the morning's events settled heavily on my chest. Blake's kiss, the way he'd held me like I was the only thing that mattered—it replayed in my mind, uninvited and relentless. And now here I was, forced to endure the day with Braxton and his endless supply of energy.

The thought made my head spin. I climbed onto the bus, the cool metal railing grounding me as I pushed my way to a seat. I had to focus. Today was about chopping potatoes and onions, not Blake, not Braxton, not the mess my life seemed to have become.

For now, this was my reality. Glamorous or not, it was all I had.

Chapter 42
Blake

The silence is thick now.

The kind that settles after a storm, the kind that doesn't let you lie to yourself anymore.

I lean back in my chair, Willow's file open before me.

The pages are too clean, too clinical to hold what really happened in this room.

The pen waits in my hand, but my fingers don't move.

Not yet.

Because I can still feel her mouth on mine. Even after all the patience I've seen today, even when the day's long over.

Session #4

Client continued discussing "Blaze" and "Razor."

Clarified prior assumption that their role was protective, instead revealing their presence serves to control her access by local males in her district. Strong signs of systemic coercion, grooming, and subjugation.

Client maintains a defiant refusal to classify her experiences as abuse, yet describes them in language that reflects deep resignation. Statements like "It's just what happens" and "I know what they want, so I use it to get what I need" reinforce internalized trauma and conditioning.

High concern for long-term emotional detachment from self-worth and boundaries.

The session became emotionally charged when the client insisted, "Don't look at me like I'm broken."

I responded with a challenging question.

She scoffed, laughing softly under her breath. She continued to tear herself down, dissecting her choices, her worth, her body—a steady stream of self-destruction veiled by a sarcastic tone.

That's when I stood. I don't even remember doing it consciously.

Frustration bubbled in my chest—not at her, but at the way she spoke about herself, like she was nothing but discarded, used, unworthy.

I told her, quietly but firmly, "If I'm not allowed to see you as broken, then you're not allowed to see yourself that way either."

And that's when I realized how close we were.

Inches.

She didn't back away.

She looked up, eyes steady, unreadable, and reached for me. A hand brushed against my shirt. A breath between us.

And then she kissed me.

It wasn't soft.

It was deliberate. Hungry. Real.

I gave in. Just for a second. My hands found her hips. Her mouth opened beneath mine. Her body leaned into mine like it belonged there.

And then, God, I pulled back.

Professional. Controlled. Measured.

I tried to breathe. To re-center. To remind myself who I was, what this role demanded of me. She needed stability, not heat.

But as I looked down at her lips, still parted… her taste lingering on mine… and then she whispered my name.

That part of me I've kept locked away, the part I swore would never surface again, was already awake. Already moving.

And I failed.

My mouth found hers again, claiming her with a force I couldn't leash. I kissed her like I needed it to survive.

And she didn't just let me—she gave back. Fire for fire.

It was only the knock on the door that ripped us apart.

Only the reminder of time, of duty, of lines we've already blurred too far.

But even now, alone in this room, she lingers.

In my mind. On my lips. Beneath my skin.

She let me in deeper today than she ever has. Spoke of sex, of pleasure, and how she's never known both to be intertwined. How it's always been currency, never connection. Survival, never safety.

But when she kissed me, it wasn't survival.

It was choice.

And I felt it in the way her body arched toward mine, not away. In the way her hands gripped me—not to escape, but to hold on.

She let me get personal today. Far more than any session before. And somewhere, deep inside, I wonder—

No, I ache—to be the first to show her that it can be different. That it can be pleasure. Surrender. Control given, not taken.

I press the pen to paper, forcing out a closing line.

Therapeutic recommendations:

Proceed with extreme caution. Client emotional disclosure increasing. Supervision recommended. Maintain professional distance.

I lock the file away.

But the walls around the beast I've hidden for years?

They're already gone.

And somehow, she's the one who shattered them, without even trying.

Chapter 43
Willow

We arrived at the soup kitchen and made our way into the large industrial kitchen. Inside, it was buzzing with the clinking of pots and the murmur of voices. The sharp scent of onions mixed with cleaning solutions lingered in the air.

It wasn't the most glamorous of places, but it would serve as my temporary escape from everything that was swirling inside me.

I headed over to our designated counter, just beginning to focus on peeling potatoes when Braxton sidled up next to me, his signature smug grin plastered on his face.

"Well, looks like we're partners for a while," he teased, his grin widening.

I glanced at him, barely managing to suppress the eye roll that came naturally. "Lucky me," I muttered under my breath, trying to keep my attention on the task at hand.

Braxton leaned in closer, that grin still firmly in place.

"Can't say I'm upset about it," he added, winking.

I gave him a half-smile, unsure of how to respond. This was… different. Something about his presence today felt oddly comforting, though I wasn't ready to admit it. And of course, he pushed further.

"Oh my gosh, Floss, is that a smile?"

Half smile.

I shot him a sarcastic look, narrowing my eyes. Braxton laughed, the sound part flirtation, part genuine amusement. "You should wear that smile more often. It's a sexy look."

The compliment threw me off more than I expected, but I couldn't help but smile back. I shook my head, "You're lucky I'm in such a good mood."

I looked him up and down, still unsure what to make of him. "I don't think even you could spoil my day."

"Wow, that hurts, Floss," he clutched his chest dramatically, like I'd dealt a mortal blow.

"Ohh! Yep, there it goes," he added, mocking, "I think I just felt my heart break in two."

I rolled my eyes, but couldn't suppress the giggle that escaped.

"Oh man, that laugh," his eyes lit up with amusement. "Damn, that's cute Floss."

I couldn't stop myself from smiling. "I'm in such a good mood that I'll let it slide that you keep calling me Floss."

"Yeah, you'll get used to it," he shrugged, his expression playful. "It suits you."

I could feel the heat creeping into my cheeks, and I quickly turned away to hide it. "It's just a nickname," I muttered, trying to steer the conversation away from anything personal.

Braxton chuckled and then went silent for a moment, clearly thinking. "So, are you a potatoes or onion girl?" he asked, his tone still tinged with flirtation.

I glanced at the pile of onions on my station and grimaced. "How about I choose the potatoes?" I scrunched my nose. "Onions make me cry."

Braxton grinned wider. "Well, I wouldn't want you to lose that gorgeous smile," he said, turning his attention to the onions.

"I'll take the sting of the onion if it means you have that smile all day."

"Yeah, yeah, keep talking, Braxton," I rolled my eyes, though a smile tugged at my lips.

"Did I just make that smile bigger?" he asked, a playful glint in his eye. I couldn't help but give in. "I'll give you that one," I muttered, though a smile fought its way through my protest.

"It was Braxton, wasn't it? I got it right?" I teased, mimicking a thoughtful expression.

"Oh, the final piece of my heart just shattered," he said dramatically, clutching his chest again. "Not even sure of my name anymore."

We both burst into laughter, and for a moment, it felt like the tension between us wasn't as heavy as before. The kitchen buzzed with the sound of chopping, but we seemed to create our own little bubble of humor.

I shook my head, still laughing. "I can't believe you sometimes."

"You know," Braxton said, his grin widening, "I think I'm starting to get somewhere with you." He shot me a sidelong glance. For a brief second, I thought I saw a genuine smile on his face.

"You're opening up," he added, nodding to himself.

I shot him a look. "I'm not like other girls."

"Yeah, I'm working that out," he said, more to himself than to me. "That's what makes you so a-peeling." He nodded toward the potatoes I was peeling. That cheeky smirk returned, I groaned, flicking a potato peel at him.

There was a momentary pause, as if he was questioning himself. Then, "So since you're talking to me today, tell me something about yourself."

I paused for a second, grabbing another potato to peel.

"My hair's pink," I said dryly, not sure what else to offer. Braxton's face lit up. "Hardy ha," he said, clearly unimpressed by the obvious. "I suppose I can put 'sense of humor' down as one of your traits."

"One of many," I replied, flashing him a sarcastic grin.

He lowered his head slightly, leaning closer, and gave me an exaggerated doe-eyed expression. "Well, hopefully, I'll find out the others."

"Yeah, in your dreams," I teased, not entirely sure if I meant it.

"Seriously, though... tell me something about yourself. What's something I don't know?"

I paused, considering the question. "Well, since you didn't like my last piece of info..." I started, then shrugged. "What do you want to know? You get one personal question."

His grin stretched wider, like a kid in a candy store. "I better use it wisely." I raised an eyebrow, waiting.

After some considered thought, he asked, "What's your favorite movie?"

My stomach immediately twisted. I froze, then quickly responded, "Nope, next question." I shook my head.

He raised his hands as if to physically stop me. "Nope. I got one question. This is the one I want answered."

I bit my lip, glancing at him nervously. "It's embarrassing," I muttered, my cheeks flushing slightly.

He looked at me with more interest and what might have been sincerity. "Now I want to know even more. Come on, Floss."

I groaned, giving in. I knew he wouldn't stop. If there's one thing I've learned about him, it's that his persistence is relentless. "You're lucky I'm in a good mood. No laughing!" I pointed my potato peeler at him.

"I promise." He plastered a serious expression on his face.

"Promise?" I sought confirmation. Not sure if I trusted him. Promises meant more to me than most people could understand. They weren't just words; they were lifelines. And the second he spoke, so casually, so unaware, I felt it—that slow sting, like pressing on an old bruise.

He had no idea how close he was to hitting something raw. Something that still ached when no one was looking.

I forced a smile, shaking my head, pretending the conversation didn't matter. Like it didn't stir something inside me I wasn't ready to face.

Because what's the point? He wouldn't get it.

And I'm not about to bleed for someone who doesn't even know I'm wounded.

This will be the first test for him.

He snapped me from my thoughts. "Cross my heart, and hope to die," he said, holding his hand over his chest with a cheeky smile.

I paused for a moment before rolling my eyes and answering quickly, almost quietly. "It's *Pretty Woman*," I cringed.

"Really?" His voice was full of disbelief.

I buried my face in my hands, trying to hide the embarrassment that flushed through me. "Don't look at me. It's embarrassing."

He grinned, clearly not as disturbed by the revelation as I expected. "Why that movie?" he asked, genuinely curious.

"You were only allowed one question," I snapped back, shaking my head.

"Well, I took the onions for you." He looked at me with mock sincerity as his head nodded towards the onions. "Don't you think I deserve a better answer?"

"You just wanted to get on my good side," I shot back.

"You got me," he admitted.

"A blind person could see that," I said, shaking my head, trying not to smile.

He smiled, obviously pleased with himself. "So, you're really not going to tell me why?"

"Nope." My eyes narrowed as I playfully teased him.

"Cold," he muttered.

"That's all you get for today, Fabio." I winked at him, giving him a taste of his own medicine.

"Fabio?" he repeated, clearly confused.

"You gave me a nickname," I mocked with my own smirk. "So, I've given you one."

"Really? Fabio?" he asked, full of disbelief.

"Yeah, it suits you," I smirked. "You think you're God's gift to women."

"Well, I can't argue with that," he flashed an infuriating grin.

Does nothing bother this man?

"Now, let's get back to peeling in silence." I snorted, turning back to my pile of potatoes. But my mind wandered briefly to the way his eyes lingered on me. We weren't so different, Braxton and I. And as much as I hated to admit it, I couldn't completely shut him out.

A few hours later, after what felt like an eternity of peeling and chopping, Frank's sharp clap echoed through the kitchen.

"Alright, delinquents, knock-off time. You've got ten minutes to gather your stuff, then it's back on the bus," he announced briskly.

Relief washed over me, the weight of the day finally starting to ease. "Time for a smoke," I muttered, rubbing my temples. A nicotine-deprived headache had been building for hours.

Of course, Braxton appeared, stepping in front of me as I made my way to the smoking area, as if summoned by my need for a moment of peace. His grin, that infuriatingly familiar one, lit up his face as he stood in front of me. "Mind if I join you?"

I raised an eyebrow at him, trying not to sound dismissive. "It's a free country, isn't it?"

He chuckled, taking my response as permission. Part of me wanted to protest, but the truth was, I didn't entirely mind the company—at least, not today.

The cool evening air greeted me as I stepped out of the soup kitchen's back door, the lingering scent of stew and the clatter of pots fading behind me. The makeshift smoking area, a quiet corner of the lot, felt like a refuge.

A battered bench sat under the weak glow of a single streetlamp, its light flickering slightly as if struggling to stay awake.

I leaned against the rough brick wall, lighting my smoke. The weight of the day still hung heavy in my chest, my thoughts swirling with everything and nothing all at once. The steady sound of Braxton's footsteps joining me broke the silence.

"So," he began, casually but edged with mischief. "What did you do to get community service?"

I shot him a sidelong glance, raising an eyebrow. "I gave you one question. You're pushing it."

He smirked, settling against the wall a few feet away. His arms crossed loosely over his chest as he tilted his head toward me. "Thought I'd try my luck."

I rolled my eyes, letting my head fall back against the wall, answering as a puff of smoke followed. "First-degree murder."

Braxton's eyes widened in mock shock. "Oh, wow, me too."

"Knife or gun?" he quipped, not missing a beat.

"Both."

His grin widened, and for a moment, I found myself smirking too. It was surprising how effortlessly he kept up with our banter. Normally, his relentless cheer grated on my nerves, but today, it felt almost… tolerable.

"Wow, I like it."

Before I could respond, the sound of footsteps interrupted our exchange. My gaze shifted toward the sidewalk, and there she was—the girl I'd seen him with at community college. Her sharp features and confident stride were unmistakable.

She stopped a few feet away, her focus locked on Braxton. "Hey, Brax," her flirtation clear for all to see.

I narrowed my eyes, trying to suppress the irritation bubbling inside me. The last thing I needed was more trouble.

Braxton straightened slightly, his attention divided between the girl and me. "What's up?" There was something in his expression, a flicker of unease, annoyance maybe, that I couldn't quite read.

"You all good to meet with Dunk tonight?" she asked confidently. "He thinks you two will make a great team."

I stepped back slightly and took a long drag on my smoke. The whole interaction set me on edge. It wasn't just the girl, but something about the way the scene was unfolding—like a puzzle I didn't want to piece together.

My gaze wandered to the empty street as unease settled over me. I didn't want to be part of whatever this was.

Rolling my eyes, I pushed away from the wall and straightened up, irritation coursing through me. I dropped the smoke on the floor, stubbed it out, and muttered quietly to myself, "And this is why we will never be friends."

Braxton must have heard me and glanced over. His expression briefly shifted, but I couldn't tell what he was thinking.

Whatever game he was playing, I wasn't interested in being anywhere near it. I pushed past him and walked through the back alley toward the bus.

Chapter 44
Braxton

I watched Willow walk away, her figure slipping into the distance like a ghost I wasn't ready to lose again. She'd finally started opening up, letting her guard down just enough to let me in. Now, it felt like I was watching her shut the door again.

I crossed my arms, masking the tension coiling in my chest. "I thought I told you I didn't want anyone knowing about this," I snapped, my voice sharper than I intended.

Roxy smirked, smug and dangerous. "Why are you worried about her?" she asked, all fake sweetness and mockery. Her soft giggle grated against my nerves, like sandpaper under my skin.

I rubbed my jaw, trying to play it off, but my thoughts were anything but calm. I could still hear Willow's voice, her laugh, the way her smile had cracked open something in me I hadn't realized was there.

"She's a dead girl walking," Roxy said flatly.

My breath caught. Just like that, my arms dropped to my sides, useless. The air in my lungs turned cold. Her words hit harder than I expected.

I stared at Roxy, trying to read her face, trying to convince myself that maybe, just maybe, she didn't mean it like that. But she did. And fuck, I didn't know how to process that.

"She upset the wrong psycho," she added with a shrug, her words echoing against the brick, each one a punch.

I shifted, my hands deep in my pockets, jaw tight as I fought to keep my cool. I hated the way her words crawled beneath my skin.

"I've heard about Razor," Roxy continued, folding her arms with a knowing smirk. "She's brutal. If I had feelings, I'd feel sorry for her."

My scowl deepened as I glanced toward the end of the alley where Willow had disappeared. My fists clenched in my pocket, my entire body tensed with the urge to chase after her. To make sure she was safe.

"Anyway," Roxy said casually, "same place at 8."

I barely heard her. I nodded without thinking.

"Maybe after, we can grab a drink," she added, tilting her head. "Get to know each other better."

I stared at her, cold. "I don't mix business with pleasure, love."

She laughed, a breathy, mocking thing that made my skin crawl. "Your loss."

She turned and disappeared into the dark, her presence finally gone, but her words lingered, like rot in the air.

My mind snapped back to Willow.

I should've been furious with Roxy. I should've gone after her. Demanded answers. More Details. But all I could think about was Willow. The worry that had twisted in my gut shifted, giving way to memories of what I'd noticed—what I'd like— about her today. That laugh. That smile. The way she made the world feel different, if only for a moment.

It had been so brief. So rare. But it had been real.

She wasn't smiling for me—not today, anyway. But I saw it. I felt it. Like the sun broke through just long enough to remind me what light looked like. That smile? It lit her up. It softened her. It made her look like someone who still had something to hope for. And those dimples, barely there, just a whisper of them, but enough for me to know they were there, hiding. Enough for me to know I wanted to see them.

I wanted to be the reason for that smile. More than I'd wanted anything in a long time.

If I have learnt anything in the short time I have known Willow, it is that she doesn't give anything away for free. She makes you earn it. And I will. I want that smile to be for me next time. And when I see those dimples, I want it to be because I earned them.

Every time she opens up, even just a little, I feel it deeper. I want to know what makes her laugh. What makes her let her guard down. I want to be the one she trusts when her world falls apart.

She makes me feel protective in a way I can't explain. It's not just about the threat Razor might pose. It's the way she looks when no one's watching—like she's bracing for the next hit life's going to throw her way. Like she's forgotten what it means to be safe.

And I want to give her that. Even if I don't know how.

Just then, something caught my eye at the edge of the alley. A backpack. Hers. Half-hidden, familiar. My pulse kicked up.

This is my chance. I grabbed it, fumbling with the straps, moving quickly. I didn't want her to see me.

Then I was off, jogging toward where she'd gone. "Hey, Floss!"

She froze when she heard me, her body stiffening. She spun, eyes narrowing, jaw tight. "You forgot your bag."

"Don't think I owe you one," she snapped, snatching the bag before I could say more. "I realized and was coming back."

Clearly, she wasn't.

There she goes—always so quick to put up her walls, not wanting to owe me anything.

I raised my hands. "Alright, alright. Just trying to help."

She rolled her eyes, muttering something I didn't catch before turning back and walking off.

I followed from a distance, back to the bus. Watching her.

And all I could think about was that laugh. That damn smile.

And the wildfire growing in my chest that told me I'd do just about anything to see it again.

Chapter 45
Willow

I turned the shower knob, and the pipes groaned in protest before a lukewarm spray trickled from the rusted showerhead. Steam began to fill the cramped bathroom, fogging the mirror and softening the sharp edges of the peeling wallpaper.

Taking a deep breath, I stepped under the stream, letting the water cascade over me, washing away the grime of the day.

Leaning my head back, I closed my eyes as a storm of thoughts and emotions swirled inside me. The memory of the day tugged at me—chaotic, full of surprises, and, most vividly, that kiss.

A faint smile ghosted my lips. The sensation of it lingered, electric and impossible to forget. My lips tingled just at the thought. "That kiss," I murmured softly, my voice lost in the steady patter of the water.

I let out a light sigh, the words circling in my mind: *I can't believe someone like that could like me.* I pressed my palms flat against the cool, tiled wall, my fingers splayed wide as the water poured over my back.

"Why me?" What could he possibly see in me? The thought clawed at me, persistent and relentless.

Shaking my head slightly, droplets sprayed against the tiles as I tried to grasp the unfamiliar sensation blossoming in my chest. *It's not like I have anything he needs.*

My hand drifted to my stomach, resting lightly as my thoughts turned to the butterflies I'd felt earlier. A shiver coursed through me—not from the cooling water, but from something deeper.

The need to be with someone. To crave them.

With a sigh, I reached for the shower knob and turned it off. The sudden silence was broken only by the rhythmic dripping of water.

Grabbing a frayed towel from the hook, I wrapped it around myself, my movements slow and deliberate as I tried to steady the whirlwind in my head.

I padded to the bedroom, slipping into soft, worn pajamas and brushing damp strands of hair from my face.

My gaze swept over the room—an unmade bed, clothes strewn across the floor, the faint clutter of a life in disarray. Kneeling by my bag, I rummaged through it, searching for a hair tie. My fingers sifted through the mess—crumpled receipts, loose change, and a lone candy wrapper—until they brushed against something unfamiliar.

What's this?

Frowning, I pulled out a small package wrapped in old newspaper. The edges were uneven, the paper fragile.

My curiosity piqued, I slowly unwrapped it. Inside was a bottle of nail polish, its vibrant pink hue gleaming faintly in the dim light. Nestled beside it was a folded piece of paper. My breath hitched as I opened the note, the handwriting instantly recognizable from college.

I know you didn't want to owe me. Floss. But we all deserve to spoil ourselves now and again. So, consider this a gift. No payback required. From your favorite community service buddy,

Brax. xx

My brows knitted together as I shook my head in irritation. *Why is he so good at irritating me?*

My fingers tightened around the note, and my jaw clenched as annoyance bubbled up.

"I can't believe he did that," I muttered, frustration seeping into my voice.

Tossing the note and nail polish onto the bed, I folded my arms, glaring at the nail polish as if it were personally responsible for my growing irritation.

If he thinks I'm going to accept this, he's dead wrong.

My thoughts churned. *It's never just a simple gift. It always means more. Always!*

Despite my annoyance, a small, unwelcome warmth flickered in my chest. The gesture was thoughtful—too thoughtful for someone like me to process easily. I pushed the feeling aside, my resolve firm. Only feelings left were annoyance: annoyance at the gift, annoyance at the confusing feelings it had stirred.

It's going back. No exceptions!

I shoved the nail polish back in my bag and climbed into bed, pulling the thin blanket up to my chin. Staring at the ceiling, the day's events replayed in my mind like an unrelenting reel—chaotic, vivid, and impossible to sort out.

Exhaling deeply, I willed my restless thoughts to quiet, though a part of me knew sleep wouldn't come easily tonight.

Chapter 46
Braxton

I pulled my jacket tighter against the night's biting chill as I stepped into the rundown trailer park. A haphazard sprawl of rusted trailers stood against the dirt and gravel, their edges illuminated only by the flicker of a faulty streetlamp. The air reeked of damp earth and lingering smoke, and the occasional murmur from inside the trailers drifted into the stillness.

My boots crunched against the ground as I approached the largest trailer. Its patched-up windows glowed faintly with dim light, and the door hung slightly ajar, creaking as the wind teased it. I hesitated, my hand hovering near the frame before stepping inside.

The interior was as miserable as the exterior. A dim, yellowish bulb cast weak light over peeling wallpaper and a sagging couch that looked older than I was. Dunk stood at the center of the room, his imposing figure dominating the space. With his shaved head, prison tattoos peeking from beneath his sleeves, and an ever-present scowl, he looked like trouble personified.

Beside him stood Roxy, her smug smirk never faltering as she gestured toward me.

"So, boss, this is Brax."

Dunk scratched his chin slowly, his sharp gaze raking over me as if he were dissecting every flaw. His silence stretched uncomfortably, but I didn't flinch.

Finally, he spoke.

"Expected you to look different," his voice carried a faint edge of curiosity.

"Different?" I raised an eyebrow.

"From what I've heard, you're fierce."

A dry chuckle escaped me. "What, I don't look fierce?"

Dunk shrugged, a shadow of a smirk tugging at the corner of his mouth. "Just different than what I pictured."

"Well, sorry I don't meet your expectations," I shot back, my voice edged with steel. "What do you want? You're the one who called this meeting. You're cutting into my main selling time."

Dunk's smirk faded as he folded his arms, his expression hardening.

"That's why you're here. You've upset some of my regulars. They say you've been stealing their clients."

I leaned back against the wall, slow and easy, letting a smirk tug at the corner of my mouth. The kind of look that said I wasn't here to play, but I wasn't about to lose either. I made sure the Glock tucked into my waistband was visible, just enough to remind them who they were dealing with.

"Hey," I shrugged, unbothered, "can't blame me for offering the kind of variety people want… at a price they can actually pay."

"That's what I've been hearing," Dunk admitted, calmly, though his narrowed eyes betrayed a hint of irritation. "And that's why I want you to join us."

I straightened, my jaw tight, eyes narrowing as I sized him up. His repositioning making his pistol visible now, tucked in his waistband.

"And why the hell would I want to do that?" I looked him dead in the eye. "I don't answer to anyone. Not some low-rent thug swinging a gun and flexing like it means something."

I took a step forward, just enough to make my point.

"All my profits are mine. I don't split. I don't share. And I sure as hell don't take orders from a meathead looking to ride my hustle."

My stare held, daring him to push it further. Because I wasn't bluffing. Not now. Not ever.

Roxy's face darkened instantly, and she stepped forward, her voice sharp. "Hey, watch how you talk to the boss!"

Dunk lifted a hand, cutting her off mid-sentence.

"Nah, I like it," he said, amusement clear in his voice. "Kid's got balls. I need more of that around here." He stepped in closer, his bulk casting a long shadow across me. The air shifted—he wasn't just talking anymore; he was claiming space.

"With your current suppliers and what I'm bringing to the table," his voice dropped low, deliberate, "you could push more. Broader reach. Better variety."

Then his eyes locked on mine, and something colder slid into his voice.

"And I wasn't just thinking about you selling, either."

My brow creased, trying to work out where he was going with this. There was something in his tone—too smooth, too rehearsed.

Dunk leaned in.

"I was thinking you could run that district for me." Everything about him was casual, like he was offering a drink instead of territory. "Get the other dealers in line. Handle the ones dragging their feet."

He paused, a smirk curling at the edge of his mouth. "Make sure anyone not pulling their weight is... taken care of. I'd only want twenty percent."

I let out a hollow laugh, short and sharp, enough to sting. "Twenty?" I scoffed, the sound slicing through the tension like a blade. "You've got a real sense of humor, I'll give you that."

I turned, boots scraping against the sticky, worn lino floor as I headed for the door.

"Alright, wait!" Dunk's voice chased after me. "Fifteen percent!"

I stopped, just long enough to glance back over my shoulder. "Ten," I smirked coolly. "And I might think about it."

Then I started to walk out—because the deal was on my terms, or not at all. Dunk crossed his arms, jaw flexing as he mulled it over. "Ten percent," he said, his voice hardening. "And I want the names of your other suppliers."

I turned to face him fully, my stare like ice. "What, for you to cut them out and leave me crawling back to you?"

He shook his head slowly, his voice steady and controlled. "Not my play. I'm building something bigger than turf scraps and egos. I bring them in, unify the supply. You get better rates, bigger margins. Everyone wins."

I rubbed my chin, eyes narrowing as I measured every word. It sounded good—too good.

"Tempting." I looked at him, narrowing my eyes, trying to read him. "But how do I know you're not just playing me?"

Dunk's lips twitched into a faint, unreadable smirk. "I'm wondering the same thing about you." He stepped closer, his gaze steady. "This deal? It's a risk, for both of us. But if it works, we both walk away with what we want."

His words hung between us, thick in the air. I studied him, every instinct firing, every part of me screaming to tread carefully.

Then I stepped in, close enough to show I wasn't backing down. My stance eased just slightly, but my voice stayed razor-sharp. "If I take this deal"—I turned to glare at Roxy—"then I need Roxy to be more discreet. I'm trying to keep a low profile."

Dunk nodded, his tone softening. "Roxy won't bother you again."

We held each other's gaze for a moment longer, taking one last moment to size each other up. I extended my hand. "Okay. It's a deal."

Dunk's grin widened, satisfaction creeping into his expression. "I was hoping you'd say that. As a starting bonus, and in good faith, here's your next supply. For free."

I took the product, our handshake solid, gritty, no-nonsense—just two men sealing a deal in a world where trust was a luxury neither of us could afford.

It wasn't friendship. It was survival.

A flicker of a smirk tugged at my lips as I met his gaze. "Who knows, might just be the start of something worthwhile."

"That's the plan." His voice was laced with quiet confidence.

As I stepped out into the night, the cold air hit my face like a slap—sharp, bracing, sobering. But it did nothing to quiet the knot twisting in my gut. No matter how smooth Dunk made the deal sound, no matter how clean he tried to wrap it up, I knew better.

This wasn't just business. It was a power play. And I'd just walked into something deeper, darker, and a hell of a lot more dangerous than I'd planned for. And now? There was no backing out. Only through.

Chapter 47
Willow

I lay on my bed, the whirlwind of the day still spinning in my mind. My heart fluttered at the memory of the kiss. No, not just a kiss—much more than that.

Turning onto my side, I reached for my phone on the nightstand. My thumb hovered over the screen for a moment. Did I dare check? Curiosity got the better of me, and I unlocked it, half-expecting a message from Blake.

My pulse quickened as I saw the notification. A message. From him. I tapped it open, and a small smile played on my lips as I read his words: "You've made it hard to work today."

I couldn't help but smile, my fingers already typing a reply, biting my lip. "How is that?"

The wait felt longer than it was, but soon his response appeared. "I haven't been able to get my mind off you all day."

Heat rushed to my cheeks as I shifted on the bed, pulling the blanket over my legs. A newfound confidence bubbled up inside me as I replied, "Is that so?"

"Yes, my mind can't stop thinking about what would have happened if we hadn't been interrupted."

My heart raced, the memory resurfacing—vivid, electric. I chewed my lip, debating my reply before sending, "Now we'll never know. I think I remember your words: 'It can't happen.' 'You're not good for me.'"

"I regret my words. Can I take them back?"

I hesitated, a teasing tone slipping into my fingers as I typed, "Not like it stopped you anyway."

"If I recall correctly, I believe you kissed me first today. I was doing my best to resist you and stay professional."

A laugh escaped me, soft and genuine. He wasn't wrong. "I'll put my hand up to that."

"Looking forward to our session tomorrow :)."

Something in me shifted—a playful boldness I wasn't used to. "I was thinking of cancelling."

"WHAT! WHY?"

"Well, you're trying to stay professional. Maybe we need a few days to cool things down."

His reply came almost instantly, his words bringing a grin to my lips. "What if I don't want them to cool down?"

I hesitated, staring at the screen. I knew where this was headed—a place we couldn't come back from. I was crafting my response when Blake broke the silence. "I've never met a girl like you before. Never has someone occupied my mind like you."

I rolled my eyes, but a smile tugged at my lips. The gesture wasn't out of frustration—it was pleasure. "I bet you say that to all the clients you fancy."

"I've never crossed a line with a client before. I've always stayed professional. But with you... I can't think straight. I know it's wrong. I'm a smart guy, but with you, logic goes out the window."

My heart raced at the raw honesty in his words. After a moment of thought, I typed back, "Maybe I'll keep the appointment then. See if we can pick up where we left off."

"I hope you're talking about the kiss and not the session."

A grin spread across my face as he reminded me about the joke I'd said earlier in our session. I sent my reply, unable to resist teasing him. "You'll have to wait and see."

"You're killing me."

"Till tomorrow."

His last message caught me off guard, surprising me yet again. "I'll have to settle for seeing you in my dreams. Night, gorgeous."

I set my phone down, my chest tightening with a mix of excitement and nerves. A squeal of delight escaped me, muffled by the pillow I pressed against my face.

A moment later, as I managed to calm down, I turned off the lamp and sank into the soft warmth of my bed, my thoughts spinning with anticipation.

A smile lingered on my lips as I closed my eyes, the possibilities of tomorrow dancing vividly in my mind.

I stood just outside Blake's office door, my hand hovering over the doorknob. The air around me felt heavier than usual, weighed down by a tension I couldn't shake.

The events of yesterday replayed in my mind—flirtatious messages, the unexpected kiss. My heart raced at the memory, a storm of excitement and apprehension. I had no idea what today would bring, but deep down, I knew it wouldn't be the usual session.

Taking a steadying breath, I turned the knob and pushed the door open. The hinges groaned, the sound unnaturally loud in the stillness of the room.

Blake stood near his desk, his back to me, adjusting his suit jacket. His stance seemed relaxed, but there was an undercurrent of tension in the air that made my pulse quicken.

"Come in," his voice was calm but carrying something deeper, something that made my stomach flutter with anticipation.

I stepped inside, the door clicking shut behind me. The sound seemed to emphasize the growing tension between us, the weight of everything that had happened—and everything that could happen.

As I moved further into the room, Blake glanced over his shoulder. His eyes lingered on me, just a fraction longer than necessary, before he turned to face me fully. The brief contact made my breath catch, and I fidgeted with my sleeve, trying to stop the nervous energy building inside me.

His gaze was intense, flickering with a mixture of uncertainty and resolve. He stepped closer, each movement deliberate, like he was weighing every action.

The air thickened around us, charged and trembling, as though the moment itself was holding its breath. Then, Blake moved, slow and deliberate, as if pulled by something he couldn't fight. He stepped in close, one arm reaching around me to the door, and I heard the faint click of the lock echo like a thunderclap in my chest.

I couldn't breathe. The sound sealed us in. Sealed this in.

My mind reeled, still spinning from the memory of our kiss— the one that had lit a fire under my skin, the one that haunted me whenever I closed my eyes. I opened my mouth to speak, unsure of the words I even had. "Blake… I…" I barely whispered.

But he didn't wait.

His hands found my waist with a confidence that stole the rest of my thoughts, lifting me effortlessly and setting me on the edge of his desk like I belonged there. The cold surface beneath me jolted through me, a stark contrast to the molten heat radiating off his body.

And then, his lips were on mine.

There was no hesitation. No second-guessing. Just raw, aching need.

His kiss wasn't soft. It was hunger wrapped in tenderness. Desperation wrapped in restraint. Every part of him trembled with the effort to stay in control and failed. And I didn't want control. I wanted this. To be wanted. To be claimed.

He stepped between my legs, his body pressing into mine, his hands mapping the curves he'd learned yesterday, like he was memorizing them all over again. I gasped against his mouth, the sound swallowed by him as his kiss deepened, rough and reverent.

I felt him—every inch of him—and it lit something in me I didn't know I had left. Fire roared through me, burning away the layers of doubt and shame I'd carried for so long. Because here, in his arms, I wasn't broken. I wasn't forgotten.

I was seen. Wanted. Craved.

But then, just as quickly, he tore himself away.

His breath was ragged, his chest heaving as he ran a trembling hand through his hair. His eyes were wild, stormy with emotions he was trying and failing to contain.

"Oh, Willow," he rasped, voice thick with regret. "I'm so sorry. I shouldn't have done that."

He stayed close, hands clenched, eyes locked on mine like he was afraid I'd vanish. "I saw you and I… I couldn't stop myself. I know I should be professional, I want to be, but you're just…" He shook his head, voice breaking. "You're too beautiful."

The ache in his voice made my heart squeeze.

A shy, uncertain smile tugged at my lips. "You took me by surprise. But… it's okay."

His shoulders sagged with relief, and then his smile, so rare, so real, broke through.

"I don't know what you've done to me," he murmured. "I couldn't stop thinking about you last night."

"Really?" I breathed, disbelief clinging to my ribs.

"Yes," he replied, without hesitation. "Really." He reached out and gently tucked a loose strand of hair behind my ear, his fingers brushing my skin like he was afraid I'd vanish if he touched me too hard.

A soft blush rose to my cheeks. "I don't think anyone's ever said that about me."

His gaze softened, something tender and fierce flickering in his eyes. He cupped my face in both hands, thumbs grazing my cheekbones. "Would it be okay…" he paused, swallowing the lump in his throat, "if I kissed you again?"

I nodded, breath catching.

And he didn't wait.

He pulled me into him, kissing me like the world had narrowed to just us. This kiss was deeper, slower, but no less consuming. His hands found the small of my back, tugging me closer until every inch of me was pressed to him.

I arched instinctively, meeting the strength of his body. He didn't touch me like I was fragile. He touched me like I was important.

Every kiss, every whisper of skin against skin, melted the edges of me I thought were gone forever. He lit me up from the inside out, and I let him. Because in that moment, there was no fear. No shame. Just the feeling of his breath on mine, the weight of his need matching my own.

And I wanted to drown in it.

Because for once, it felt like I was exactly where I was meant to be.

In his arms. Wanted. Chosen. Alive.

Chapter 48
Blake

Every time she walked into my office, the man I pretended to be—the professional, the polished, the in-control version of myself—started to unravel. Slowly at first. Then all at once.

Willow didn't just tempt me.

She provoked me.

Not with intention, never with games. No, she did it by simply existing—quiet and guarded, with fire in her eyes and bruises on her soul. She was stunning, yes, but that wasn't it. It was her stillness. Her strength hidden beneath the surface. The way she tried not to be seen, when all I could do was look.

And want.

Every rule I set for myself before our sessions shattered the moment she entered the room. Her voice, soft, hesitant, wrapped around my name like it belonged there. And it did. God help me, it did.

I told myself this couldn't happen.

That it must not happen.

I've been here before—too close, too raw, too reckless. And it nearly ruined me.

But Willow isn't like the last one. She isn't venom dressed in affection. She isn't manipulation in disguise. No, she's fire trying to survive in a world that keeps drowning her. And she keeps burning anyway.

She's been mishandled. Dismissed. Used.

And I would rather burn than be another man who adds to that.

The beast inside me, controlled for years, silenced, caged, stirs when she's near. He doesn't want her out of lust. Not just that. He wants to possess her. To protect her. To claim her from the world that's done nothing but fail her.

And that thought should terrify me.

It doesn't.

It grounds me.

Because for the first time in years, I want to give someone more than fragments of myself. I want to hand her everything—my darkness, my restraint, my hunger—and trust that she won't run.

And if she does?

I'll wait.

Because Willow is not someone you chase for convenience. She's someone you earn. One stolen glance at a time. One moment of trust after another. She deserves to be seen, not stripped. Held, not handled. And I will be the one to give her that.

Because I choose her.

Not for what she's done. Not for how she makes me feel. But for who she is—raw, real, unfinished.

I'll be the man who rebuilds what they tried to destroy. Not out of pity. Not to fix her.

But to make her better. Because she deserves to feel what it means to be wanted, not used. Claimed, not owned. Loved, not tolerated.

She won't get the shattered, compartmentalized version of me the rest of the world does.

She gets the truth.

The heat.

The beast.

All of me.

That's not just a feeling.

It's a vow.

And it starts now.

With one decision.

To no longer resist what's already mine.

Chapter 49
Willow

The intensity of Blake's kiss lingered on my lips, igniting a wildfire beneath my skin. Passion surged through me, tangled with a flicker of uncertainty, but it didn't stop me from leaning into him, wanting more. Every touch sparked something wild and electric, something I couldn't name but craved deeply. His presence overwhelmed everything else—his need thick in the air, impossible to ignore. And God, I wanted him too.

My hand slid up his chest, feeling the rapid thunder of his heartbeat beneath my palm. I wanted him to know—I was here, with him, ready. My fingers drifted lower, brushing over the metal of his belt buckle, uncertain but full of intent.

But he stopped me.

"No, Willow," he said firmly, taking both my hands in his. Not with rejection, but with restraint, like something barely leashed inside him couldn't afford to be set free.

The words hung between us, making my heart stumble. Had I read it wrong? Shame prickled at my skin, but before it could take hold, his hand rose to my cheek, gentle. His thumb brushed softly across my skin, grounding me.

"If you're okay with it," his voice was raspy and breathless, "I want today to be about you."

When I met his eyes, the rest of the world fell away. The sincerity there hit me so hard it almost hurt, like something too good to be meant for me. But it wasn't just sincerity I saw—there was desire, raw and undeniable. And something else, something I could not name, but felt all the same. It wrapped around me like a promise I didn't know I was waiting for, and suddenly, I wasn't sure where I ended and that feeling began.

"I don't want to be like the other guys," each word heavier than the last. "You're special, Willow. I want you to feel that."

Something shifted inside me. Not just the heat between us, but something deeper. His words felt like truths I'd never known how to believe in—solid, grounding, dangerous in the way they made me hope.

His hands slid down to my waist, deliberate, commanding. My breath caught as his fingers hooked beneath the band of my pants. There was no hesitation in him. Every movement was sure, like he was in control of the moment—and of me—without question. The cool air kissed my skin as he pulled the fabric away, and for a second, I froze.

But his eyes... that look. Dark, intense, unwavering.

"Trust me, Willow," he murmured.

And I did.

I nodded, my heart hammering. Then his lips were back on mine—slow and deep—and everything else fell away. His touch was purposeful, each motion coaxing something deeper from inside me. When his hands pressed gently against my thighs, sliding up, I shivered uncontrollably.

No man had ever touched me like this. Not with such care. Not with such focus.

A moan slipped from my lips, and I felt him smirk against them, a brief, satisfied curve of his mouth before he kissed down my neck. Each press of his lips was tender, but behind it was something stronger. He wasn't asking for permission anymore.

My body responded like it belonged to him, arching, aching, desperate to be touched.

His kisses slowed, deepened, each one leaving a trail of fire. My breath caught as he lowered onto his knees, eyes never leaving mine until he pressed a feather-light kiss over the soft cotton between my thighs. My entire body jerked at the intimacy of it—breathless and undone.

Then he moved the fabric aside. Slowly. Carefully. Like he was savoring every inch of skin he uncovered. Like this wasn't about pleasure alone, it was about claiming. Attention. Focus. Me.

And when he touched me, his mouth on me, his hands anchoring me in place at my hips, I shattered.

It was overwhelming. Amazing. My fingers found his hair, anchoring myself to him as waves of sensation took hold. He moved with control, with purpose, guiding me into surrender—unraveling me piece by piece.

The sounds that spilled from me weren't things I recognized—soft, broken cries I didn't know I could make. My back arched, body trembling, lost completely to him. There was no shame in it. Only him. Only this.

And when the final wave tore through me, all I could do was collapse against the desk, my breath jagged, my body humming with aftershocks.

Blake didn't speak.

He didn't need to.

His hand rested against my thigh—possessive and steady. And in the stillness, in the way he looked at me like I was his to protect, to worship, to claim...

I felt more alive than I ever had in my life.

I didn't know what this was becoming. I didn't have the words for it. But something inside me knew this moment meant more than anything I'd ever known before.

I was his. And I didn't even realize it.

Chapter 50
Braxton

The sun beat down relentlessly over the skate park, the heat shimmering off the pavement. The air buzzed with the sounds of grinding boards, spinning wheels, and the occasional cheer when someone landed a trick.

I leaned casually against the edge of the park, arms crossed, scanning the skaters with idle curiosity. Beside me, Ray stood with his usual sharp, watchful gaze, though his posture seemed relaxed.

A short kid with messy orange hair hovered nearby, completely absorbed in his phone.

"I told you, I'm just not interested."

I smirked, this only presented a challenge. I liked nothing more than challenges. I could be very persistent when there was something I wanted. "What can I do to change your mind?"

Ray shrugged, his patience clearly wearing thin. "I'm happy with the way things are."

I arched an eyebrow, a hint of amusement creeping into my voice. "I'm sure I can change that, make things better."

Ray let out a sigh, glancing away toward the park, his arms folding tighter across his chest.

"Isn't there something you want that you're not getting?" I pressed, trying to coax him into playing along.

Ray didn't bite. His focus was zeroed in on the scruffy orange-haired freckly kid, still glued to his phone.

"Come on, man, there's always something."

"I don't think so," he muttered without even looking in my direction.

Before I could push further, the kid looked up from his phone, yelling at another boy across the park. "No, I can do it better than you!"

Ray's attention sharpened. A flicker of thought crossed his face. "Hold that thought," a faint grin forming as he turned to me. "You can help me with this."

I tilted my head, intrigued. "Help you with what?"

Ray gestured toward the grocery bag in his hand, stuffed with bread and milk—an odd sight for a man of his trade at a skate park.

"If you can get this kid to take the bread and milk off me," his voice carrying a note of challenge, "then I'll do my next order with you."

I frowned, puzzled. "Who carries bread and milk around with them?"

Ray shrugged. "I do... because of this kid." He nodded toward the scruffy orange-haired boy, now back to staring at his phone.

I laughed, shaking my head. "I don't do the whole kid thing, man."

Ray rolled his eyes, exasperated. "No... no, dude, it ain't like that. It's his sister."

Relief washed over me. "Thank the heavens for that," I muttered. But curiosity gnawed at me. "So, what's the deal?"

Ray's expression grew serious. "They need help, and he's always suspicious. I just want to get on his good side... for his sister. I like her, man. I just want a chance with her."

A sly grin spread across my face. "Well, I can help a man out there."

Ray nodded, his resolve firm. "If he takes the stuff, we've got a deal."

"Bring it on," I grinned, rubbing my hands together, accepting the challenge. "I'll have that deal."

Ray called out, "Noah!"

"No," Noah grumbled without even looking up from his phone, flat and uninterested.

Ray tried again, more insistent. "I want you to meet my friend."

Noah sighed, clearly annoyed, but walked over anyway. He gave me a quick once-over, his scowl deepening.

"What do you want?" Noah asked, arms crossed, impatient. Ray gave him a warm smile. "Me, nothing. But..." He gestured toward me. "My friend Braxton wanted to meet you."

I waved with a friendly smile. "Hey, Noah."

Noah rolled his eyes. "What do you want?"

I shrugged, trying to seem casual. "Just wanted to say hey."

Noah didn't buy it. "Hey. I'm going now." He turned quickly to return to where he had been sitting.

"Hold up," I held up my hand quickly to grab his attention. Noah sighed but stopped, turned, and glared at me. "What?"

I hesitated for a moment before asking, "Could you do me a favor?"

"Nope," Noah instantly shook his head.

I glanced at Ray for backup, but was getting nothing. So, I turned my attention back to Noah. "Guess you were wrong, Ray. He ain't a tough guy."

Ray shrugged, feigning indifference. "Sorry. Thought he was up for it."

Noah stiffened. "I'm tough."

"Sure," I raised an eyebrow. "But I was hoping someone big and responsible could help me out."

Noah straightened, pride flickering in his expression. "I'm big and strong."

I smirked, sensing my opening. "Well, I bought too many groceries," I held up the bag. "If I take them home, my girlfriend will know I spent too much, and I'll get in trouble. I don't want to throw them away. That would be wasteful."

Noah's eyes darted toward the bag, curiosity lighting his face. "I could take them."

Caught off guard by his quick response, I blinked. "What?"

Ray chuckled. "That would fix your problem, and mine."

I grinned, shaking my head. "You'd do that for me, dude?"

Noah nodded, smiling. "Barb's eaten all ours. We need food badly."

As Noah walked off with the groceries, I turned to Ray, a teasing grin on my face. "So, I can expect a call for your next supply?"

Ray smirked. "If your girlfriend is okay with that."

"Haven't got one, but I'm working on it."

I shot him a playful look. "Good luck with his sister."

Ray winked. "Oh, I don't need luck now, thanks to you."

I laughed as I adjusted my stance, watching Noah jog off. Something about today felt like it was going to work out in my favor.

Chapter 51
Willow

I struggled to steady my breath, my chest rising and falling in short, uneven bursts as the fire he'd ignited within me began to cool. But, my cheeks burned, the weight of what had just happened crashing down all at once. I felt bare—not just undressed, but exposed. Laid open in a way I didn't know how to process.

I covered my face with trembling hands, shame pressing against my ribs. Was this normal? Was I normal for letting it happen? I'd never felt anything like this before, and now that the desire filled haze was lifting, all I could feel was heat rising up my neck and confusion twisting tight in my gut.

Blake noticed, of course. He always noticed. With quiet, calm confidence, he adjusted my clothes for me. The way he moved was careful, slow, and controlled. Like even now, especially now, I was something precious in his hands. Then he leaned down and kissed my forehead—a simple gesture, but it jolted me. The warmth of it sent a ripple through my chest.

"There's no need to be embarrassed, Willow," he murmured, his voice rich and low, like a promise made only for me.

I didn't know how to answer. I couldn't. My thoughts were too loud, too jumbled, and all I could do was breathe and hope he didn't see how messy I was inside. Was this what he meant when he asked about pleasure? About sex for me? Because nothing about this felt like what I'd known. It felt... bigger.

Blake gently pulled my hands away from my face, coaxing me to look at him. His lips curved into a soft smile, and he pressed a gentle kiss to my lips—not rushed, not demanding. Still in control.

But his control didn't ease the flush in my face.

I met his gaze briefly, then looked away, cheeks burning. He stood there, effortlessly composed, running a hand through his tousled hair. He looked like he had done this a hundred times before—calm and sure. Like he knew exactly what I needed, even when I didn't.

"Now, what's that look for?" curiosity apparent through his voice.

I shrugged, the knot of confusion in my chest too tight, too tangled to pull apart. I didn't know how to put it into words—the strange mix of comfort and ache that came with being wanted. The warmth of it, the way it filled me up, and the sting of not knowing what it truly meant. To be seen like that, laid bare in front of a man, letting him glimpse that part I usually keep hidden… it was too much. Too overwhelming.

"I know you enjoyed that," he added, his voice velvet over steel. There was reassurance in it, but something else, too. Something that made me feel small and cherished all at once.

I bit my lip, still unsure. But I nodded faintly. His smile widened—not arrogant, just sure. Like he'd expected nothing less.

He gestured toward the couch. "Why don't you sit for a bit?"

I moved slowly, my limbs still unsteady, and sank into the cushions. He followed, sitting across from me, posture relaxed but watchful. The air between us had shifted. He had changed it. Claimed it. Claimed me, in some way I didn't know how to define.

"We have twenty minutes left of our session," his voice was quiet.

"Okay," I whispered, still swimming in the aftermath.

He leaned forward slightly. "Do you mind if we talk? So, I can get to know you better?"

I hugged my knees to my chest, curling inward. "Okay."

The silence stretched, the only sound the soft hum of the air conditioner. I didn't know what to do next. I didn't know what people did after something like that.

Something so intimate.

Blake tilted his head. "What do you want to talk about today?"

I glanced up at him, a small, uncertain smile flickering. "What do you want to talk about?"

He chuckled under his breath. "Anything you want."

"Ask me anything," I offered, voice low. "I'll answer the best I can."

He nodded, his tone shifting. "Have you received any more threats?"

I sighed, fingers toying with the edge of my sleeve. "I ran into that guy the other day, but… nothing you need to worry about."

His jaw flexed. I saw the tension there. "Have you called the police?"

A bitter laugh escaped me. "They said they can't protect me. The detective said they'll be locked up until the trial, so I guess it's just talk."

Blake leaned in, eyes darkening. "Let me know if anything else happens."

"I will," I nodded, though I wasn't sure I meant it.

A silence settled again—softer, but heavier.

"Do you want to talk about your foster mom?" he asked.

I hesitated. "What do you want to know?"

"How long have you lived with her?"

"Two years."

His expression was unreadable. "You said she's not good to you. How does she treat you badly?"

I clenched my hands. "She doesn't care. As long as we show up to department check-ins so she gets her money, she's fine. She spends it on smokes, pokies, whatever. I had to work with Razor and Blaze to keep food in the house."

His face darkened. "Without Razor and Blaze, how will you make money?"

Frustration bubbled up. "I don't know. I've got community service. College. No time for a job. And who would hire someone like me?"

I watched his hand move to his back pocket. He pulled out his wallet and offered me a twenty.

"Take this. It'll help."

I stared at it. My chest tightened. "I can't. That's not why I told you."

"I know." His voice stayed soft, but there was something underneath. Something that didn't take no for an answer.

My stomach turned. Anger flared. "You said you didn't want to be like the other guys." My voice cracked. "Giving me money after what we just did? You are just like them."

His eyes darkened with regret and something else. Something that felt dangerous. "It's not like that."

I crossed my arms, pulling back. "You're just like them."

He ran a hand through his hair, jaw clenched. "I made it clear earlier, I'm not. I shouldn't have these feelings. I definitely shouldn't be acting on them."

Then his voice dropped again, gentler now. "Are you really going to hold it against me? That I want to help the woman I care about?"

My breath caught. My chest squeezed. *Care about?*

"If people find out, I could lose everything. But I don't care. I have no agenda, Willow. Just the need to know you're okay."

He took my hand, turned it over, and pressed the note into my palm.

"I know you don't trust it yet. That's okay. Just keep it. If you don't spend it, and you get by, you can give it back. No strings."

I stared at the crisp bill in my hand, speechless.

Then, a knock at the door.

He exhaled and stood, rubbing a hand down his shirt. "That's my next client." He turned toward the door, then glanced back. "See you tomorrow."

I didn't speak. Didn't know how.

I stood there, silent, for a moment, then stormed out.

I was furious with him. So angry after everything that had happened, and everything I had told him. Then, after what just happened, for him to go and give me money? He should have known better. If he really wasn't like everyone else, he should have known better.

But I had to get to college. I had the rest of the day to get through.

Chapter 52
Blake

The door closed behind her.

She didn't slam it.

Didn't even look back.

But her silence was louder than any goodbye.

I sat at my desk, waiting for the next client to enter, the air thick with everything I had just done right—and everything I had just ruined.

My fingertips pressed against my lips. Her taste still lingered.

And God… the way she sounded.

The moan that slipped out of her mouth when my tongue found the right rhythm. The way her hips trembled beneath my hands. The way her body melted into pleasure—real pleasure, for the first time in her life.

I know it was the first.

I felt it in every gasp, every twitch, every soft, desperate whimper she tried to hold back and couldn't.

And for one brief, brilliant moment, I was the one to give her that.

Not to take. Not to trade.

But to give.

She was shy afterwards, of course she was. Cheeks flushed, eyes wide, hands flying up to cover her face like she didn't know what to do with that much feeling. That much trust.

She tried to laugh it off, but her body gave her away—legs still shaking, hands trembling against her thighs. My hands. My mouth. My control.

I relished it.

Because it meant I reached a part of her no one else ever had. I was careful. I was patient. And I earned that moment.

I earned her.

It should have been perfect.

And then…

I stuffed it up.

I opened my mouth.

Said the wrong damn thing.

The worst possible thing.

We talked about Barb. About how she never cared for them, how she never fed them, and how Willow no longer did scouting or stealing to help feed her sisters and brother. I gave Willow money.

I thought I was doing the right thing.

I didn't think about the last session. About what she said.

"They give me food because they want something back."

And what did I do? I gave her pleasure, then I handed her money. I practically stepped into the same shape as the men who treat her body like currency.

No matter how pure my intent, no matter how fiercely I want to provide for her, to look after her, to make sure she never needs another man again, it doesn't matter.

She thinks I'm just like them.

And I saw it.

In her eyes.

She didn't yell. Didn't lash out.

But the moment changed. The air around her thickened. Her jaw tightened. Her gaze, once soft and vulnerable, iced over in an instant.

She was angry.

God, she was furious.

And she had every right to be.

I didn't mean to betray her trust. I just wanted to make sure she was fed. That she had something, anything.

But all she saw was control. Another man crossing lines. Another man doing what he thinks is right, without asking her what she needs.

That's on me.

Even though I gave her everything today—every ounce of care, of gentleness, of pleasure—she left thinking she'd been bought.

Like the others.

I close her file.

There's nothing I can write tonight that won't feel like a lie or a failure.

I'm not sure what damage I've done.

And I don't know how to fix it.

But I do know this: I will. I have to.

Because she's not just another client.

She's herself.

And she's cracked open something in me I never thought I'd let live again.

And I won't lose her.

Not like this.

Chapter 53
Willow

The air feels heavy, thick with the tension that's been clinging to me since the therapy session with Blake. His touch, his eyes filled with sincerity—those still linger in my mind. But then… the money. It shattered everything, turning whatever fragile connection we had into something I don't know how to process.

I sit slouched in one of the worn chairs at the back of the classroom. The desk in front of me is cluttered with open textbooks, a blank notebook, and a pen that I've been absently tapping against the wood. The lecture drags on, but I'm not listening. My mind is replaying the events from Blake's office on a relentless, torturous loop.

The scrape of a chair against the floor snaps me out of my thoughts. Braxton slides into the seat next to me, his usual cocky grin plastered across his face.

"Hello, beautiful lady." He's clearly in a playful mood, oblivious to the storm swirling inside me.

I roll my eyes, irritation bubbling up before I can stop it. It's instinctive now—his cheerfulness grates on me like sandpaper against raw skin.

"Wow, where's the happy-go-lucky Floss from yesterday?" he teases, leaning closer and nudging my arm with his elbow.

I barely glance at him, my expression flat. He doesn't get it. No one does. Men are all the same. I don't have the energy for his shallow jokes or his attempts at charm.

Braxton scratches his head, clearly puzzled by my lack of response. He lowers his voice, leaning in as if we're sharing a secret.

"Come on, Floss, we had so much fun yesterday."

His words are a jab to the wound I've been nursing. The memory of Blake's office rushes back—fleeting connection, crashing down with the twenty-dollar bill. My grip tightens on my textbook as if I can physically keep the memory at bay.

Braxton doesn't let up, his tone now a mix of teasing and coaxing.

"Come on, where's that sexy smile?"

That's it. I've had enough. A sharp, sarcastic sigh escapes me. My patience snaps. I look at him, fire in my eyes.

"Will you shut the fuck up?" My voice cuts through his attempts at banter like a knife.

He shifts beside me, the air between us suddenly tense. His usual bravado falters.

"I'm not in the mood to talk today," I continue coldly. "So, take the fucking hint."

I turn away from him, trying to shut him out, but of course, he sees it as a challenge.

"That look ain't sexy at all," he mutters. I hear the hint of concern creeping into his voice, but I'm too mad to care.

I whip my head back toward him, my glare sharp enough to cut. He doesn't understand how desperately I need silence.

"And while I'm at it…" I reach into my bag, pull out the nail polish he bought me, and toss it at his chest. It lands with a soft thud—the motion almost satisfying in its release of pent-up frustration.

"Take your damn nail polish back. I don't want it."

He stares at me, his cocky demeanor slipping. For the first time, he looks unsure of himself, rubbing his chest where the bottle hit him.

"Man, you're making it hard," his response quieter now.

I don't stop to think. The irritation, the anger—it all boils over.

"Hard to what?" I snap.

"Hard to be your friend and be nice to you." His voice is soft, laced with real concern, but I'm too far gone. Braxton is just the latest person to absorb everything I've been holding in.

A bitter laugh escapes me, sharp and hollow. "Friends," I mutter, the word tasting sour. "I've had enough of them. They only bring pain."

I narrow my eyes and say, in my iciest voice, "I don't need friends."

I see his expression soften, and for a second, I think he might actually understand. But then he ruins it, just like everyone else.

"Everyone needs friends, Floss."

I shake my head, frustration bubbling over again.

He doesn't get it. No one does.

"They've brought me nothing but trouble in the past," I say bitterly. "You won't be any different." My eyes narrow, rage building.

I turn away, crossing my arms tightly over my chest, determined to shut him out. I need to focus on this class—not on him, not on Blake, not on the mess in my head.

"Now shut up and let me concentrate," I snap, trying to sound as authoritative as I can. "I need to pass this class and get out of this shithole."

I stare at the front of the room, my eyes fixed on the lecturer, though I can't process a single word she's saying. My heartbeat pounds in my ears, drowning out the world around me.

But no matter how hard I try to focus, I can't escape the confusion swirling inside me or the echo of Blake's actions.

Chapter 54
Braxton

I lean back in my chair, sneaking subtle glances at Willow. Her posture is stiff, arms crossed tightly over her chest like armor. She's not just annoyed—there's something deeper, something raw in the way she sits, staring ahead like the world's pressing down on her. It's like she's fighting some invisible battle and has no intention of letting anyone see it.

Man, she must be having a bad day. Usually, she's sharp, brimming with energy that could cut through steel. But today? That spark is gone. Instead, she's barricaded herself behind walls even thicker than usual.

Yeah, she's pissed. Anyone can see that. But I don't think it's all directed at me. Still, it's impossible to ignore the intensity of her mood. It's frustrating, sure, but at the same time… it's kind of fascinating. That fire in her—*even when it's scorching everything around her*—is magnetic. She doesn't even realize it.

I try to think of something, anything, to break the tension. But what could I possibly say? She's giving me absolutely nothing to work with. She's stubborn and proud, and if I push now, it'll only make things worse and could end any chance of me getting to know her at all.

Willow isn't like anyone else I've ever dealt with. She keeps people at arm's length like she's daring them to try and get close. But even if someone manages to earn her trust, I'm not sure she believes anyone's worth the risk. It's maddening. And intriguing.

I glance down at my textbook, pretending to focus, though the words on the page might as well be in another language. Willow's been ignoring me the entire session, and while part of me is relieved not to be dodging her barbs, the silence feels wrong. Normally, there's some kind of exchange between us, even if it's just her finding new ways to shut me down. Today, it's like she's checked out completely.

My mind drifts to the nail polish. She tossed it back at me without a second thought, like I didn't even deserve an explanation. I wonder if she thinks I'm just another guy who's going to disappoint her. Is that what she sees when she looks at me? Just another let-down in a long line of them?

The teacher's voice drones on, blending into the background as I steal another glance at her. There's something about her resistance that gets under my skin, no matter how many times I tell myself to let it go.

Any other girl, I would've moved on by now. I don't usually bother with the ones who put up walls this high. I go for the easy laughs, the ones who smile at my jokes and don't make me work too hard for it. But Willow's not like that. She doesn't need anyone, and from what I can tell, she doesn't want anyone either.

And yet... here I am. Still trying to figure her out. Still wanting to break through the walls she's so carefully built.

I don't know why. Maybe it's the way she challenges me, making me second-guess everything, or maybe it's the way she hides her vulnerability so well that it feels like a rare treasure, something no one else has ever seen. Maybe I want to be the one she shares it with. Be that lucky one.

Whatever it is, I can't shake the feeling that there's more to her than she lets on. And for some reason I can't explain, I'm determined to find out what it is. If she thinks she can push me away that easy... she is mistaken.

Chapter 55
Willow

Finally, it was lunchtime, and I found myself alone in the secluded nook I had claimed as my own. The distant clamor of the cafeteria was muffled here, offering the peace I craved. I unwrapped my half-sandwich, savoring the rare solitude, hoping it would give me the clarity I desperately needed.

At least I could count on this place for quiet. No one really ate lunch out here, so I could almost always guarantee some time to myself.

I sighed, my thoughts circling back to what had happened in class. Guilt gnawed at me as I reflected on how I'd treated Braxton. Maybe I'd been a little too hard on him. It wasn't really about him—my confusion about Blake had spilled over, and Braxton had just happened to be in the line of fire. Still, he had a knack for pushing my buttons.

A faint rustling snapped me out of my thoughts. I looked up and saw Braxton emerging from the bushes, his expression a strange blend of casual indifference and that familiar smugness. His hands were stuffed in his pockets, and he stopped a few feet away, studying me with a slight tilt of his head.

"Ah, so this is where you hide out," he said, his face absent of his usual cocky smirk or cheeky grin.

I straightened in my seat, gripping my sandwich tighter. "What do you want?" I asked curtly, locking eyes with him. "I thought I made it clear how I felt earlier."

He leaned against the tree, a faint smile playing on his lips. "I don't know if it's the way you went off on me, or just a gut feeling, but I get the sense you're having a bad day."

I dropped my gaze to my sandwich, biting back the instinct to snap at him again. "You might be right," I muttered. "Doesn't mean I want to talk to you."

"Wow," he stood upright, feigning surprise. "And you think I want to talk to you after that display back there? I just wanted somewhere quiet to eat my lunch. Is that okay with you?"

I waved a hand dismissively, my irritation softening just slightly. He stepped closer, settling down on the edge of the nook, keeping a respectful distance. He unwrapped a bagel, eating quietly as though trying to blend into the stillness around us.

I glanced at him out of the corner of my eye, fiddling with the crust of my sandwich. A pang of guilt settled in my chest. I'd been harsh. Maybe too harsh. With all the emotions already swirling inside me, I didn't want to add guilt to the mix.

"I'm sorry," I muttered, barely above a whisper.

He didn't react, continuing to chew his food as though he hadn't heard me.

Clearing my throat, I said louder, "I said I'm sorry."

He turned to me at last, eyebrows raised in exaggerated surprise. "Are you talking to me?"

I rolled my eyes, regretting the decision to apologize. Of course, he wasn't going to make this easy. "Yes, I'm sorry," I repeated, more sharply.

He leaned back, feigning deep thought. "Sorry?" he echoed. "Can't think of anything you could possibly be sorry for."

"You're not going to make this easy, are you?" I mumbled, glaring at him.

He shrugged, his expression daring me to continue.

I sighed, relenting. "Look, I'm sorry I bit your head off earlier. I'm having a bad day, and I shouldn't have taken it out on you. I still don't agree with the nail polish thing, but I could've been nicer about it."

He tilted his head, letting my words linger in the air for a moment before nodding. "Apology accepted."

He returned to his lunch without another word, his easy demeanor catching me off guard. I expected a smart remark, maybe some teasing, but there was nothing.

Resting my chin on my hand, I studied him. That didn't go the way I'd expected. Where was the usual teasing? The "Floss" nickname? I can't say I wasn't grateful, but it made me curious. Why had he dropped the usual bravado? Could he actually realize that I wasn't up for it today?

He seemed to sense my gaze but didn't acknowledge it. Instead, he pulled out his phone and scrolled idly, his expression unusually neutral.

A sudden vibration in my pocket pulled me out of my thoughts. I fished out my phone, frowning as I saw the caller ID. My pulse quickened as I answered hesitantly. "Hello? Yes, this is Willow Anderson."

The voice on the other end identified itself, and my chest tightened.

Detective Pierce.

"Why are you calling?" My voice rose, frustration spilling into my tone as I stood and began pacing in tight circles. "You said they wouldn't get out! You said there was no bail. They've already threatened me!"

I pressed a hand to my temple, closing my eyes against the surge of panic. "Can you offer any protection?" I demanded.

The answer was the same as before: no.

"I know you said you couldn't," I rasped through gritted teeth, my voice sharp with desperation. "But she threatened me. She said she's going to kill me so I won't testify."

The call ended abruptly, leaving me staring at the phone in disbelief. "Well, good day to you too, Detective," I muttered bitterly, shoving the phone into my bag before slumping onto the bench.

Braxton, who had been pretending not to listen, frowned.

He hesitated for a moment before pulling out his phone again. "Hey, it's me," his voice dropping to a low murmur. "Yeah, everything's fine. I need a favor."

He moved farther away, his voice too low for me to catch the rest of the conversation. But to be honest, I had more pressing things to worry about than whatever trouble he was getting into.

Chapter 56

Braxton

I stepped away from Willow, just far enough to be out of earshot, my body instinctively angled to shield the phone. My voice dropped, rough with urgency. "I need you to look into someone—Willow Anderson. She's doing community service, but something's off. I overheard her on the phone... someone's threatening her. I need to know everything. Call me back."

As I ended the call, a heavy exhale tore from my lungs. The words she'd said still echoed in my head, raw and panicked. This wasn't a slip-up. She wasn't overreacting. It was real.

This wasn't just some run-in with trouble. This was serious. Life-threatening.

I turned, searching for her, and there she was, pacing the edge of the clearing like she couldn't breathe unless she was moving. Her steps were sharp, agitated, like her skin didn't fit right anymore. The anger she wore earlier had melted into something else. Fear. It clung to her like a second skin.

And I felt it. Deep in my chest. Like it was my own.

Watching her unravel like that—someone so clearly used to walking through fire without flinching—gutted me. Whatever storm she was in, she wasn't just bracing for it. She was drowning in it.

I ran a hand through my hair, forcing myself to stay grounded. Her apology from earlier still lingered in my mind, soft around the edges. It had taken effort for her to say those words. Vulnerability like that? It hit different. It was real. And I felt something shift in me the moment I saw it.

But this, what I was seeing now, this was more than just regret. This was survival mode. She wasn't mad anymore. She was scared. Terrified.

My fists clenched at my sides. I hated standing here doing nothing. I hated the way my chest ached every time she glanced over her shoulder, like she was expecting something, someone, to appear out of nowhere. I wanted to cross the space between us, wrap her in my arms, and promise her she was safe. That I'd make damn sure of it.

But I didn't. I stayed still.

Because she wouldn't let me.

Not yet.

And I knew pushing her would only make her build the walls higher.

So, I stood in silence, watching her steps falter, her head drop, like the weight of her fear had finally settled into her bones. When she turned to head back inside, her movements had changed. Slower. Heavier. Like she was dragging a thousand invisible anchors behind her.

I followed, but from a distance. Close enough to step in if something happened, far enough not to make her feel cornered.

When she slipped into the seat beside mine, she didn't look at me. Her shoulders sagged, her hands curled tightly in her lap. She looked like someone who'd stopped trying to carry her world and just let it collapse around her instead.

I shifted slightly in my chair, just enough to watch her without making it obvious. Usually, Willow carried herself like she was untouchable—brave, sharp edges, and grit. But now… now she was small. Folded in on herself. Her fingers tugged at the sleeve of her shirt with quiet desperation, over and over again.

I'd never seen her fidget.

She was barely holding it together.

I watched the rise and fall of her chest. Slow. Measured. Forced. She wasn't just breathing. She was trying not to break.

What the hell is going on with you, Floss?

The thought pulsed through me, heavy, fierce.

Then my phone buzzed.

The call.

My stomach twisted as I glanced at the screen. The room felt too quiet. Too slow. I raised a hand to the teacher, barely looking away from Willow.

"Sorry," I murmured. "I need to take this."

And without waiting for permission, I was out the door. Not because I didn't care.

Because I cared too much.

Chapter 57
Willow

I trudged along the cracked sidewalk, the late afternoon sun casting long shadows over the uneven pavement. My bag felt heavier than usual, and my thoughts churned restlessly, an unrelenting storm.

"Floss, wait up!"

I froze at the sound of his voice. Of course, Braxton. He always seemed to pop up at the worst times. I sighed, not bothering to look back, and kept walking, but his footsteps grew louder, faster, gaining on me.

"Willow, wait!" He jogged to catch up, his breathing uneven from the effort. I stopped abruptly and turned just enough to glare at him.

"What do you want, Braxton?" My voice sounded tired, even to me. "I'm not in the mood."

He hesitated, scratching the back of his neck. His tone softened, unexpectedly sincere. "Let me walk you home."

I shook my head, already turning away. "I can't do this now, Braxton. I've got a lot on my mind."

His persistence was evident as he stepped closer. "Stop being so damn stubborn and let me walk you home," he insisted, his voice firm but not unkind.

I crossed my arms, halting in my tracks and facing him fully. I narrowed my eyes, giving him a hard look. "I'm not stupid, Braxton. I know you're not doing this out of the goodness of your heart."

His expression remained unchanged, calm and steady. "I'm not after anything, Willow. I swear. I just think you need some company today."

I let out a resigned sigh. "Fine," I muttered. "I don't have the energy to argue with you. If you want to follow me, there's nothing I can do about it."

Braxton's lips twitched into a smirk. "And there it is." I added dryly. He rubbed the back of his neck, looking almost sheepish. "Come on, let's go."

We fell into step, him trailing a pace behind me as the road stretched on. The silence between us felt heavy, but I barely noticed the sound of heels clicking closer until a voice broke through the tension.

"Brax, wait up!"

I glanced over my shoulder to see the same girl from the past few days striding toward us, her glossy hair bouncing with every step. Braxton turned around, irritation flickering across his face.

"I'm busy right now. What do you want?" he snapped, crossing his arms in a defensive posture.

I rolled my eyes but didn't engage. Instead, I stayed silent as the girl sauntered closer, unfazed by Braxton's sharp tone.

"Dunk's got a message for you," her voice smooth.

I could see Braxton's jaw tighten. "I thought I told you I wasn't dealing with you anymore."

I didn't care about their exchange. While they went back and forth, I seized the opportunity to slip away. My legs carried me quickly down the sidewalk, purposeful and determined. I didn't glance back. I had enough trouble on my plate without adding more.

"Dunk says…" Braxton's voice snapped impatiently. "Tell him I'll call him later tonight. I've got something more important to do." The gap between us widened, and their voices grew fainter.

I turned the corner, my heart pounding—not from fear, but from exhaustion and frustration. The last thing I needed was Braxton tagging along, no matter how persistent he was. I just wanted to get home, without any distractions.

A few moments later, I heard his familiar voice in the distance, panic clear as he realized I was gone. "Come on, Floss! Where did you go?"

The girl's voice followed, mocking. "Looks like 'dead girl walking' is immune to your charm."

"Shut up and leave me the hell alone," I heard Braxton shoot back.

I didn't wait to hear the rest. My feet carried me faster down the quiet street, away from Braxton, away from everything. The wind picked up, brushing against my skin as I moved toward the solitude of home—or whatever counted as home these days.

I slipped into an alley, the narrow path cloaked in shadows from the towering buildings on either side. My heart pounded, each beat frantic and erratic.

I paused, taking a shaky breath, trying to steady myself.

Looks like the coast is clear. I glanced over my shoulder, scanning for any sign of movement. The alley seemed empty. Quiet. Too quiet.

The silence pressed in on me, suffocating. I forced myself to keep moving, the sound of my own footsteps echoing softly against the cold brick walls.

Then, I heard it. A voice. Low, mocking, and all too familiar.

"Well, what do we have here?"

I froze. My heart stuttered before kicking into overdrive, a frantic rhythm pounding in my chest. Slowly, my eyes darted toward the voice. My breath caught in my throat as two figures emerged from the shadows, their movements deliberate, predatory.

At first, they were just dark shapes, but as they stepped closer, the weak daylight filtering into the alley revealed their faces—the ones I had prayed never to see again.

Razor and Blaze.

Razor's grin stretched wide, predatory and taunting, as she crossed her arms over her chest. Blaze trailed behind her, her stance cold and rigid. Her expression was as hard as stone, offering no mercy.

"Thought I could smell a rat," Razor's voice slithered out, deadly. She tilted her head toward Blaze, never breaking eye contact with me. "And what do we do to rats, Blaze?"

Blaze smirked, her lips curling in a way that made my skin crawl. "Exterminate them."

A cold, constricting weight pressed against my chest. The air around me felt thick, suffocating. My lungs burned, each breath shallow and ragged. My legs felt frozen in place, even as my instincts screamed at me to run.

They closed in. Razor's grin grew sharper, her eyes gleaming with cruel satisfaction. Blaze followed, her gaze unwavering, locked on me like a predator savoring its prey.

This isn't happening. It can't be happening.

The glint of something metallic caught my eye—Razor's knife. My stomach churned as the realization hit.

They said nothing as they advanced, the silence between us hanging heavier than their words.

Step by step, the distance between us closed. I forced myself to move, taking a shaky step backward. Then another. My boots scraped the pavement, the sound too loud in the otherwise quiet alley.

Their eyes stayed fixed on me, unrelenting. Razor's smirk deepened, her fingers flexing as if testing the knife's weight. Blaze remained unmoving, her cold stare promising only pain.

My throat felt dry. My voice was lodged somewhere deep inside me. I couldn't speak. I couldn't cry for help. All I could do was retreat, my trembling hands clutching my bag's strap like it could protect me.

The look in their eyes... I knew that look all too well. There was no doubt. No hope. I was a dead girl.

I continued to back away, my steps faltering as the alley closed in around me. Razor twirled the knife now, the blade flashing in the weak light as she toyed with it, her gaze fixed on mine. Each slow movement was a silent threat.

Blaze cracked her knuckles, her body as still as stone. Their deliberate approach felt like a noose tightening around my neck.

I kept moving, my legs trembling beneath me, but the escape I had hoped for now seemed impossibly far away.

Then, I felt it—the hard, unforgiving wall pressing against my back. My breath hitched, faster and more frantic. There was no escape. This was it. These were my last breaths.

Razor's face curled into a cruel grin as she stepped closer, her eyes shining with something wicked. Her voice came low and gravelly, like it had been dragged through every bad thing she'd ever done. "We're gonna gut you like the pig you are," she spat.

The words hit me like ice water, but it was Blaze's laugh that made my insides twist. She stood beside Razor, calm and giddy, as if this were just another game to her.

"But first," her voice dripped with malice, "we're gonna have some fun."

Before I could even register the threat, before I could move, scream, or breathe, I felt it.

Not pain—at first. Just… cold. A strange, hollow kind of pressure blooming low in my stomach. I looked down, everything slowing as if time had slipped underwater.

The knife. Razor's knife. Its blade was sunk into me, right into the soft part of my gut. The metal caught the light, dull and wet, and my mind just froze.

I couldn't breathe. I couldn't feel. My body registered the shock before the agony.

"Think you can rat us out and walk away?" Razor snarled, her voice trembling with rage. Then she twisted the blade. And the pain exploded. White-hot. Blinding.

A ragged gasp tore from my throat as my hands shot to her arm, weak, trembling, useless. My knees buckled. The world tilted sideways. But she didn't stop. She didn't even blink.

The worst part? They didn't just want me gone.

They wanted me to suffer. And I could feel it. This time, I might not come back.

Razor's smile wasn't just cruel—it was intentional. A slow, deliberate thing that stretched across her scarred face like she was savoring every second of what she was about to do.

"Stop..."

The word barely escaped, more a breath than a plea, strangled by the swelling pain in my throat.

But she didn't stop. She pressed harder. I felt the blade sink deeper, sliding into me like it belonged there—as though it had been waiting for this moment. My body buckled forward instinctively, arms wrapping around my stomach in a futile attempt to protect what had already been taken.

My hands came away soaked in blood—hot, sticky, real. The sight made me dizzy. Terrified.

Blaze's hand clamped down on my shoulder, jerking me upright before I could brace myself.

She slammed me back against the wall, hard. My head snapped back, a sharp crack of pain at the base of my skull sending stars spinning across my vision.

"You're not going anywhere," she spat, her grip bruising, eyes alight with something gleeful and vicious.

I looked down. Blood was everywhere now, soaking through my shirt, trailing down my legs, dripping onto the pavement like it was spelling out how this would end.

Razor watched, twisted joy on her face. Her smirk widened as my breath came in shallow, shuddering gasps.

"What's the matter?" she taunted. "Got nothing to say now?" Blaze's laugh rang out, cold and jagged—like nails scraping across my skin. "You had plenty to say to the detective the other day."

My heart dropped. They knew. Of course, they knew.

"Oh, are we not friends anymore?" Razor mocked, her voice dripping with a saccharine sweetness that was anything but kind. Her eyes didn't soften, not for a second.

She turned to Blaze, feeding off the moment, ignoring the silent plea for mercy in my eyes—the kind I knew I wouldn't get.

"Do it, Razor!" Blaze snapped, practically vibrating with excitement. Razor turned back to me, her smirk a razor's edge. "You were so happy to spill your guts the other day," she sneered, venom lacing her words, as her eyes gleamed.

"Now I get to enjoy watching you spill them."

Before I could even process her words, the knife tore through me, slicing across my stomach in one brutal, unrelenting drag.

It felt like my soul was being ripped out, a white-hot slash that stole the air from my lungs. I jolted, every nerve screaming as fire and ice collided in my gut—burning and freezing me alive all at once.

My mouth opened, but no sound came. No scream, just the ghost of a breath that wouldn't come. I looked down, and the sight turned my blood to ice.

The knife was still buried to the hilt. My shirt soaked through with crimson. My skin split wide.

A cold wave of dread swept over me, crashing through the heat of the pain, pulling me under. My whole body trembled violently, my knees buckling, but I didn't get to fall.

Blaze was still gripping me. Holding me upright.

Forcing me to stay in it. To feel it. To watch it. To break.

Tears spilled down my cheeks before I could stop them—hot, fast, desperate. I hated them. Hated that they showed how close I was to shattering. Hated that they showed *them* my vulnerability. But I couldn't hold them back. Not this time.

The pain was too much. It had taken everything. This is how it ends. The thought slid in quietly but stayed. Cold. Final.

My world began to dim at the edges, color bleeding into dull gray, the shapes around me softening, melting. My vision tunneled, black creeping in like smoke from a fire I couldn't put out.

And through it all, I heard Razor's laughter—sharp, wicked, distant. It sounded like it was coming from underwater, echoing in my ears long after her lips had stopped moving.

Even as the darkness swallowed me, even as my body gave up, one thought burned through it all.

Noah.

His face flashed through my mind like a flare in the dark.

His scruffy hair. His crooked grin. His freckles. His innocence in a world that didn't deserve it.

Would he be okay? Would he know I did this for him?

The questions gripped me harder than the pain.

I wasn't ready to let go. Not if it meant leaving him behind. But the answers—those answers—they were slipping, fading, disappearing with the light.

And I was sinking.

Thank You!

From the bottom of my heart, thank you for taking the time to read *Wicked Games*, my very first novel. I hope you enjoyed getting lost in Willow's world as much as I loved writing it.

Your support means everything to me, and I'd love to hear from you! Flick me a message on Instagram (@hope_epi) or TikTok (@hope_everly_) and tell me:

- *What did you love most about Wicked Games?*

- *Who has your heart—Blake or Braxton?*

- *What do you think will happen next?*

Your thoughts, theories, and kind words inspire me to keep writing. Thank you for being part of this journey.

If you wanted to also help out an independent author writing a review on good reads is another way to get the word out about me and my books.

With love,
Hope

About the Author

Hope is an Australian romance writer who crafts raw, emotional stories about survival, second chances, and the complicated path to love. She began writing in 2017, on an animated story app, as a way to escape the realities of chronic illness and found her voice in characters who are broken but brave. After a breast cancer diagnosis in 2024, Hope returned to writing with a renewed passion—and a promise to tell stories that make readers feel deeply.

Wicked Games is her debut novel, born from her own journey of healing and hope. When she's not writing, Hope can be found daydreaming new plot twists, drinking coke zero, or doing fun activities with her family.

My social Media:

| Instagram: | TikTok: | Facebook |
| @hope_epi | @hope_everly_ | Hope Everly |

Website:

https://hopeeverly.company.site